Standish O'Grady

In the Wake of King James or Dun-Randal on the Sea

Standish O'Grady

In the Wake of King James or Dun-Randal on the Sea

ISBN/EAN: 9783743398139

Manufactured in Europe, USA, Canada, Australia, Japa

Cover: Foto ©Andreas Hilbeck / pixelio.de

Manufactured and distributed by brebook publishing software (www.brebook.com)

Standish O'Grady

In the Wake of King James or Dun-Randal on the Sea

IN THE WAKE OF KING JAMES

OR

DUN-RANDAL ON THE SEA

IN THE WAKE OF KING JAMES Or DUN-RANDAL ON THE SEA

By STANDISH O'GRADY
AUTHOR OF "FINN AND HIS
COMPANIONS," ETC.

London * * * J. M. DENT & CO.
Philadelphia * J. B. LIPPINCOTT
COMPANY MDCCCXCVI

Printed by BALLANTYNE, HANSON & CO.
At the Ballantyne Press

CONTENTS

v

vi CONTENTS

DUN-RANDAL ON THE SEA

CHAPTER I

DUN-RANDAL ON THE SEA

I STARTED—drew rein—and stared in silence.
Never had I seen peel, tower, or castle weather-
stained to such a dismal hue. Blacker than
blackest coal, it seemed cut out as with a
giant's scissors from that gleaming panorama
of sea, land, and sky. A sandy plain engirdled
the base, a grey bewildered sea the waist ; the
battlements showed clear and stark against
wild clouds lurid with sunset.

Truly, I was no antiquarian. Picturesque
antiquity had no worshippers then. We did
not think of castles as romantic, only as uncom-
fortable dwelling-places occupied by the poorer
sort of gentry ; for no one lived in a castle who
could afford to build a house. In the mixed

A

emotions with which I gazed at Dun-Randal, the thought of poverty, perhaps of extreme poverty, played its part.

So I stared at the black keep starting solid black and minatory from the grey shore. Here the Atlantic had thrust inland a great tongue of barren sand. At the base or root of this tongue rose the dismal keep which was the goal of my long journey, the seat of my nearest surviving kinsman, Sir Theodore Barrett, the acknowledged head of a family once powerful and famous, but upon which disaster in many forms had long sorely beaten.

I perceived that the grim keep was the last link of a chain of castles which at some remote time, with their connecting curtains, ran across the base of this delta of sand. Between it and the juncture of grey sand with tawny grass westward lay several sandy mounds, out of which here and there ruinous black masonry struggled to view. Upon that tawny shore, a stone's throw from the sand, but in a straight line with those heaps, rose a low, square house, thatched. It resembled the basement and one storey of some great and strong castle transformed to modern uses. Indeed, I had no doubt that this was the last link towards the west of that chain of which the black tower was the first. There was a courtyard attached, with offices, but the whole seemed deserted or uninhabited. A scrubby wood, blasted by the breath of the Atlantic, and stripped barer by early winter, tried to screen, but could not, the nakedness of that sad group. In fact, everywhere desolation seemed to reign; the boom of the Atlantic raging afar against an iron coast sounded in my ears, and the low moan of the long waves rolling over the sand. All life seemed to have been arrested here; neither men nor cattle were visible anywhere. The whole scene suggested some wild tale of magic and enchantment. A coward physically I certainly was not. I don't remember having ever shown the white feather where any ordinary or natural demand was made upon me; but this night my mind was fretted and disturbed, filled with fears of I know not what monstrous and unnatural forms of evil. The physical aspect of the country through which I had been all that day riding had, I think, predisposed my mind to the entertainment of such alarms. Born and reared in fertile, rich, well-wooded Meath, in the midst of green pastures, lowing cattle, white and golden corn-fields, abundant husbandry, and abundant vegetation—a country inhabited by a prosperous peasantry and an affluent gentry, where the best forms of civility known in Ireland prevailed—a land of great trees and castellated mansions, where in winter the kine gave more milk than they elsewhere did in summer—a land of cuckoos, of flitting bats in the eventide, of the soft complaint of the wood-dove, I had been all this long mournful day riding past uncouth and horrible mountains, huge savage protuberances of ill-disguised stone, showing mysterious clefts and gashes in their horrid sides ; past melancholy bog-lakes, on which pale lilies swam weak and wan and ghost-like ; past desolate swamps, where little white fluffy things shook always to the faintest wind, and where from time to time I caught sight of "naturals," who seemed wilder and weirder than even the dismal country which they inhabited. Of the houses which I had ridden past, some seemed deserted. From the doors of. others scared faces watched me. Such faces, too, started up from behind rocks, suddenly disappearing if I looked in their direction. More than once a raven flew over my head ; then I would listen to his ominous voice croaking steadily, and tapering away till it merged in the great silence. Some mysterious curse seemed to brood over the whole region. Could my cousin— mine—be lord of this mournful and nigh empty land, a land over which, as I knew, the waves of our wasting civil war had never rolled. For it was the far west of Ireland, held— down to the date of the treaty of Limerick— by the lords and gentlemen who adhered to the cause of the late king, James II. ; and since the treaty and the sailing of Sarsfield and the Jacobite army for France, there had been peace on all sides. And at the end of this melancholy ride suddenly I came as it were face to face with Dun-Randal on the Sea, the climax of a growing mystery, nay, to me, though not one of the fearful sort, the climax of a gathering terror.

The poor beast upon which I had ridden since morning, and who seemed a moment before dead-beat with travel, appeared to watch the scene with as much interest as myself. Her erected ears and general air of alarm caused

me to smile, and recalled me to myself. I
shook away that irrational and almost superstitious feeling, and contemplated the scene
anew. An island of unusual formation—for
it resembled some great fish lying motionless
upon the water—rose out of the sea about a
mile from the root of that sandy tongue, its
head, so to speak, looking eastward. The
western extremity was forked or divided, com-
pleting that curious resemblance to a fish. It
was black-sided, and streaked tawny and grey
on the back. How little I then foresaw the part
which this island was destined to play in the
singular adventures which were to befall me
during the ensuing se'nnight. Looking again
to the right and north, my eyes sweeping past
the grim keep and that chain of ruined towers,
I perceived, at the extreme tip of the sandy
tongue which curved round a little towards
the west as it ran inland, a little hamlet of
thatched cabins.. There was no living thing
visible there, nor any sign of smoke.

Shaken off for the moment, that sense of the
preternatural returned upon me. The absolute emptiness and desolation which involved
all things, while there was so much of·human

handiwork visible, was curiously disturbing to the imagination. No note of any song-bird indeed reached my ear; and yet the scene was not without its own melancholy music, for there sounded at intervals the crying of curlews, and, shriller and more piercing, the fugitive and elusive calling of unknown birds as they flitted in little flocks to and fro over the grey strand, while the dull booming of the breakers far away and the long roar of the waves on the sand never ceased. A cormorant took flight from the shore-rocks, and, beating the water with his wings, flew seaward. Singular how I remember that swart ungainly bird when so much else has been expunged from memory, and with what distinctness, at this moment, after so many years, I can recall his ominous-looking form and flight.

But, after all, it was upon the castle itself that my eyes were chiefly directed and my thoughts centred, standing out there in the midst of that grey desolation so strong and minatory, dominating, as it were, all this sorrowful region in its grim power.

No rampart wall or bawn encircled it. No offices or any builded adjunct broke the bare

outlines of its ebon regularity, ascending there
black, sheer, and naked from ‚the grey sand,
which lay heaped around its feet, blown in
mounds there, driven thither by blowing winds.
No sign of human life was visible within or
around ; no smoke ascended from the battlements of the dark tower.   The only living thing
which I could anywhere perceive was a solitary
female figure sitting motionless with bowed
head upon the sand, a black spot in the midst
of all that grey desolation.

CHAPTER II

RAPPAREES, GOOD AND BAD

I HAD never met my cousin. We had taken opposite sides in our civil war ; for while I and many of my neighbours had served under King William, Sir Theodore and his sons had fought for King James during both the Irish campaigns, like loyal, if mistaken, gentlemen. In this war, as in so many others, all Ireland was divided, some taking one side, some another. I have known not only brothers and cousins, but fathers and sons who were engaged on opposite sides, according as the love of liberty or the traditions of loyalty might happen to prevail. My cousin and his sons had chosen, as I believed, the wrong side; they had certainly chosen the unsuccessful one, and were, as I had little doubt, now sick of their loyalty.

Singularly enough, Sir Theodore was associated in my mind rather with thoughts droll and whimsical than any other. One of the few

things which I could recollect about my father
was how he used to laugh at the Christian
names which "cousin Theo" had bestowed
upon his sons, viz., Enoch, Israel, and Immanuel, and how he would ring all sorts of
merry changes upon those extremely Scriptural
names, while my sweet mother sat silent, and
could not join him in his merriment, though
she would try. Divided from them by nigh
the breadth of Ireland, I had seen nothing and
heard little of my west-country cousins. I
knew that they had lived much on the Continent, had returned to Ireland during Tyr-
connel's Viceroyalty, and had fought for King
James in the two Irish campaigns. One of
them I knew, Immanuel, had been publicly
commended by the Duke of Berwick for his
gallantry at the Boyne. Yet their politics notwithstanding, the Barretts, as I have mentioned,
were my nearest surviving kinsmen ; and as I
was about to serve King William in the Low
Countries, no sooner had I received Sir Theodore's invitation to visit him at Dun-Randal,
than I determined, peace having been restored,
and all highways, as was thought, cleared of
rapparees and loose people, to spend a few days

with my unknown Jacobite kinsfolk in the west
before turning my back upon Ireland, perhaps
for ever, following the king of my choice to his
foreign wars. Nor was I now journeying to
visit these victims of mistaken loyalty empty-
handed or giftless, for I knew that, always poor,
and pursued by many disasters and calamities,
the event of the war just closed might well
have reduced them to sheer want. In a leathern
girdle clasped round my waist I carried a sub-
stantial store of guineas, and in my breast a
heart as charged with kindness and goodwill
towards my Jacobite cousinry in the far west
as my girdle was with gold bearing the joined
effigies of my king and his beautiful queen.
Judge, then, of my feelings when at the close of
a ride so dismal as that which has been suggested I, who had been cherishing so many
almost boyishly pleasant and agreeable thoughts
and hopes concerning this visit, stood at last
face to face with this black, ominous, and for-
bidding keep, Dun-Randal on the Sea.

I was alone. At the last posting station I
had been unable to get myself a horse-boy.
When my destination became known the
various lads and young men who had at first

volunteered their services one after another
seemed to have discovered highly plausible
reasons why they could not accompany me.
I had arrived so far by simply following the
directions of the master of that posting establishment, a grim, dour, and silent man, who,
when I spoke of Sir Theodore and of Dun-
Randal, closed his lips fast, and exhibited a
countenance as hard and inscrutable as granite.
Yet I could not mistake the way : a single
horse-track led almost from his door, some
twenty miles eastward, to the black tower,
which my heart told me was Dun-Randal.

For the last two hours I had not exchanged
salutation or speech with any living wight,
save two wretches in ragged Jacobite uniforms,
who, at a point some twelve miles rearward,
had challenged me, not with very satisfactory
results to themselves.

They stood a little off the highway hard
by a poorish sort of thatched cabin in the
entrance of a defile. The matches of their
firelocks were alight and smoking. They were
rapparees seemingly, and no pleasing speci-
mens of their type.

My response could not have been much

to their minds, for ere they could guess my purpose I had them both covered with my two long holster-pistols, which I had taken the precaution to keep at full-cock, and had so disposed that I could pluck them forth in a trice. I bore some treasure on my person, and those were times in which wise travellers were wont to be on their guard.

"Master Hugh Netterville," I answered, in reply to their challenge, "late lieutenant in his Majesty King William's third regiment of Irish Foot, and I travel the straight road to the house of my kinsman, Sir Theodore Barrett, of Dun-Randal on the Sea." There was indeed little courage in this prompt action and frank speech ; only the sheerest prudence, combined perhaps with a little presence of mind. Had these rogues been right Jacobite soldiers, I might not have dared to take such a liberty with them. For contrary to what I hear on all sides of me just now, I hold that the drilled Jacobite Irish soldiery of the civil war were in no respect second to any. At present I believed that the only safe way of dealing with such rascals as the rapparees who had challenged me was to cow them with a bold front.

One of them, with a ridiculous assumption of military ease and precision, replied sonorously, "Pass on, Master Hugh Netterville." "Not until you drop your matchlocks, my friends," I answered, with as intimidatory a look, as I could assume. "So! And you shall both walk abreast with me for some distance up this glen."

They did so, with faces like hanged dogs, till I dismissed them, returned my pistols to their holsters, and rode forward. Had I acted otherwise, I strongly suspect that a brace of bullets through my back would have been the result. Since then I had not met or seen any one save those scared, peering faces to which I have referred, which in a land so desolate made things seem almost spectral, and as though my ride into the west-land were some vivid and fantastic dream.

Were these cutthroat-looking ruffians my cousin's men? Was I about to step within some deeply devised snare? Was the letter a forged document and decoy, the work of some secret enemy? If so, my retreat was now barred. The rascals whom I had come over by my quickness, and dumfoundered by my sudden audacity, would take care not to be caught off their guard a second time, should I now, yielding to my thick-coming suspicions and the ugly and ominous appearances rising on all sides, determine to retrace my steps and ride back out of this accursed country.

While my attention was divided between the rueful spectacle before me and such thoughts as these, I heard behind me the sound of manly voices and the steady tramp of marching feet, noises to which I listened with a faculty of hearing sharpened by so many dim alarms and apprehensions. The sounds which now struck my ear were quite unexpectedly agreeable and reassuring. Two men, soldiers as I guessed, young, brisk, and fearless, were marching after me out of the now darkened east. I could not see them ; but the sound of footfalls may, to one who listens well, convey a great deal of meaning. In my present state of mind there was to me something very welcome in that honest military tramping. Not for a single instant did I suspect that it arose from the shambling hoofs of my late rapparee acquaintances, or of men in the least resembling them.

Two advancing figures now took shape in

the gathering gloom, and rapidly approached. I faced my horse round to meet them. As I did so the two men brought their hands to their caps with a military salute, using at the same time the customary Gaelic salutation, which in English may be expressed, "God and Mary be with you, O gentleman." (Dhe ás Wirra dwith a dhinna oosal.)

One was a powerful athletic youth, with lips as yet untouched by the razor, eyes bright and bold, and hair of a bright red. He was not handsome, but of a fresh, honest, pleasing, and withal soldierly aspect. His companion was smaller, lighter, and more alert. Both strode along with a certain military air of fearlessness and *sang-froid*. They were not in uniform, nor did they carry matchlocks, only short straight swords in plain scabbards, swords which rang pleasantly with a faint music in their loose sheathings as the young men stepped briskly along. The smaller of the two held in his hand a little leathern wallet, such as a skilled workman might use for the portage of tools. They were certainly a refreshing contrast to the two dirty and skulking fellows who had challenged me in the pass.

The taller and more athletic of the pair gazed at me for a moment with a keener scrutiny than I relished, and then suddenly looked away, but with a certain pleased, I almost thought amused, expression, as if he would hide a smile.

" Have we met before ? " I asked.

" We have *so*, your honour. I was in the Bog of Aughrim, and be the same token your honour was dressed in green and gold, and leading a file of blue Williamites, and not four perches from me where I stood, with my gun in my hand, and the same loaded and at the cock and to my shoulder."

"And you had a shot at me too, you rascal, I'll warrant," I said, laughing, for the wars were over.

" Sir, I'll tell no lie," he replied. " My captain he says to me, ' Pick him off, Conahar, the big young officer in green and gold facing the Blues and speeching them,' meaning none else but your own self, sir. And says I to myself, pressing the trigger, 'That same now would be a pity, seeing he's that young and *clever*, and his face too much to my mind, and he with his back this minute to the bitter stroke of death.' And I steered past

B

your honour right-wise and shot a littler one
that was behind, in green and gold too, whatever contrairy thing brought you both into
the Blues at that time ; and he was a black
and bitter one, too, for all his green and gold,
meaning no offence to you, sir, being a war-
comrade of the same.   And my captain, be the
same token, damned my ‘ crooked finger ’ for
me.”

"Then I suppose I owe you something,
Conahar,” I said, laughing still ; "for though
you seem to have shot a brother officer, and of
the same regiment, I cannot say that he was in
any sense my friend.”   So saying, I brought
my hand to my pouch.   To my surprise, however, the youth refused my intended gift, and
with a decisive gesture.

"You paid it already, sir, in full ; for in the
races I heard your honour cry loud to the
Dutchmen to give us quarter.   And I owe it to
your honour and no one else that my ugly face
isn’t looking at the roots of the daisies this
blessed night.   And what makes you, sir, for
to be in these outlandish places to-night, if I
might make so bold ?”

"I visit my kinsman, Sir Theodore Barrett,”

I replied. "Yonder black tower, I take it, is Dun-Randal—Dun-Randal on the Sea."

He stopped, suddenly faced round, and looked at me. I was walking my horse at the time with the soldiers marching one on each side. I stopped too, almost involuntarily, and looked at him.

"I'm thinking your honour is a stranger to the Barretts?" he said, after a long pause.

"That is so, Conahar," I said. "I never met them, or saw them in my life. Sir Theodore, hearing that I was about to go abroad, kindly invited me to spend a few days with him at Dun-Randal."

That Aughrim story was, I believed, true. I too now at sight felt the same sort of liking for him which singularly enough even in the heat of battle he seemed to have conceived for me. I desired to indicate as much by my frankness and communicativeness, which might otherwise seem a little out of place. Indeed, to tell the truth, I felt very kindly disposed to both these young martialists.

"Fall back, Brian," he cried, with a certain authoritativeness, to his companion, who obeyed the order with military promptness.

Conahar now came close up to my stirrup, and knitting his brows and lowering his voice, said with much earnestness—

"Sir, guard yourself well in Dun-Randal. It was for no good they brought you here. For, I take it, you're not one of their soart."

So well-meaning seemed the youth's face, so plausible his manner, so natural was it that after our singular *rencontre* on the field of Aughrim he should concern himself in my welfare and set me on my guard against possible foes, and so much in harmony with my dim apprehensions did his speech seem, that I did not for a few seconds quite realise that I was hearkening to very vile insinuations urged against my own kinsman by a perfect stranger. I was silent, but only for a moment.

"Enough," I said sternly, "not one word more. I believe you are an honest fellow, but also that you are the victim of some delusion, and, in brief, and to deal quite frankly with you, I cannot listen to such language concerning a gentleman of my blood."

Bidding him a cold farewell, to which, however, he responded with another respectful salute, I set spurs to my horse and rode down the western slope of the ridge abutting upon that strand, and by a bridle-track which, as I guessed, led to the black tower. The stars were out now. One star of surpassing lustre shone just above the dark battlements ; it was the evening star, the radiant planet Venus.

CHAPTER III

THE WATCHER BY THE QUICKSANDS

WHEN I was a young man the obligations of kinsmanship were far stronger than they are to-day. I have known many a man take the field in order to avenge a slight cast upon one who was no further related to him than that he bore the same surname. It was, in fact, impossible for me, as a gentleman and a man of honour, to hold any further converse with this young soldier, though I liked him. And yet, as I rode forward and alone down the sloping ridge along the bridle-path leading to the grey strand and the black tower, I was sorry that honour forbad me to hold further colloquy with the young man who called himself Conahar. What did I know of the Barretts, though they were my kinsmen ? Nothing. At the point where the road, or, to be more accurate, the bridle-path, met the sand there was a long bridge, or rather causeway, spanning a quicksand. This quicksand was the work probably of a descending inland stream, which here percolated through the sand. At a certain point about half-way across the bridge, the handrail had been broken through on the left. Hard by the spot where the bridge terminated on the firm sand sat that solitary female figure which I had before observed from the crest of the ridge. She looked up when my horse's hoofs began to thunder upon the timber of the bridge. Her face was pale and still, pure-complexioned, with great eyes, gentle as a fawn's, and full of sorrow. Yet it was a sweet and fair face too, that of a girl who, as I judged, was still in her teens, and had seen and known little of the wickedness of the world.

"What do you here, my girl, in this lonely place?" I said kindly. I was interested by her beauty and forlorn situation; also in the present troubled state of my mind I desired, so far as I might with honour, to learn all that was possible about Dun-Randal on the Sea before that gloomy fortalice should gather me in. Indeed the words, and especially the manner, of that young soldier called Conahar had alarmed me. "What do you here?"

"Waiting for the general Resurrection and the Day of Judgment," she replied.

She said it quite simply, and like a little child. Her voice was low and sweet, and, like her countenance, of a refinement which seemed to suggest that she did not belong to the peasant class. I started, as well I might. The poor thing was insane.

"Who lives in yonder black castle ?" I said, pointing with the butt of my riding-whip at Dun-Randal.

In the same simple, quiet tones, regarding me gently, she replied, "The Great Dhoul and his sons."

I sprang from the saddle, and walked towards her, leading my horse.

That too loquacious youth who called himself Conahar might have entertained an unjustifiable animus against my cousin, derived from some family feud, or originating in sheer perversity ; but this poor creature was different, plainly a simple, innocent, and trustful soul, driven mad by some great wrong.

"How have they wronged you ?" I said.

She pointed to the quicksands, just below

where the fractured spikes of the broken handrail showed white in the moonlight.

"My man is there," she said. "It was the Great Dhoul's second son, Israel, that did it, he and his angels. My man knows I'm here. He talks to me sometimes, always with the flowing tide. Hark now," she said, bending forward and inclining her ear to the ground. I heard nothing but the roar of the long waves as they rolled ceaselessly up the level sand.

"What does he say?" I asked.

"Have patience, Evish, Evisheen *dhuv dheelish* (little Evis, dark, sweet), 'tis I who am not far from you. The Lord Himself, high and mighty, is coming; He is on the road, and the ropes are spun and twisted for the hanging of the Great Dhoul and all his children. Be ready, Evish, for at the first note of the bugle I will come to you, my two arms around you, and my mouth to yours for ever and ever."

Thinking it cruel to put any further questions to the poor creature, I bade her a gentle farewell, and leading my horse by the bridle, slowly walked over the sands towards the black tower.

It will be admitted that, to hear my own

cousin called "the Great Dhoul" even by a
daft woman, was no exhilarating circumstance,
coming as it did at the close of such a day,
commencing with the refusals of the horse-boys
to bear me company, and concluding with
what I have described ; and the reader will
appreciate the absence of alacrity with which
I drew nigh to the great black tower, the seat
of my Jacobite cousinry, now looming between
me and the stars. As I paced beside my tired
steed over the faintly gleaming sand, Dun-
Randal seemed to wax and wax until it assumed
monstrous proportions against the starry sky.
It seemed by its own mass and force to be
dragging me towards it. The huge black keep
looked as if it would incorporate me too in
its own sinister being. All through, too, the
moaning of the sea, of the waste, wild, and
savage Atlantic, to me an uncouth mystery,
the aspect of the grey-white barren sands, the
sense of desolation, the crying and piping of
the flitting night-birds, and many other doleful
sights and sounds, increased my growing reluc-
tance to set my foot within that dismal tower.

While, nevertheless, I pausing advanced and
advancing paused, I heard behind me sounds

the most mundane—the sturdy thumps and reverberation of my soldiers' honest tramping feet upon the bridge. I doubt if there is anything more wholesome, more a natural foe to superstitious fears and all misgivings and apprehensions of such a character, than the noise of smitten and sounding timber. Timber is the honestest of things. The perfume of cut fir, the noise of the woodman's axe, and the rip of his cross-cut, would purify the uncanniest glen in the unholiest night of all the year. Truly, in the vast and weird silence which reigned here, the dull thunderings and thumpings of those well-shod martial feet exercised a strangely reassuring effect upon my shaken and fluttering imagination.

"Evisheen, pulse of my heart," cried a manly yet tender voice, which I recognised as Conahar's, "God and Mary be with you, pretty one, for sad and lonely is your post this night."

As I had halted, the Jacobites were soon at my side.

Again the respectful military salute. Said Conahar, who seemed to bear me no malice, "Your honour, I'm thinking, will be in want of some one to take the naig, give her a rub down, a drink, and a handful of oats, the crayture, and send her home by a safe hand."

"My kinsman's people will, no doubt, attend to all that," I replied ; for I had not yet quite forgotten the ground of quarrel. "You are quick steppers," I added.

The young man who called himself Conahar divined, I have no doubt, my secret desire to renew the conversation.

"There is no one in the castle," he replied, "barring the big lame man who never leaves it, for sorra a light is there in Dun-Randal this night; and, for sure, Sir Theodore and his sons are abroad."

Though it was now quite dark, save for the moon and stars, no light showed anywhere in the black tower. It rose up before us a black rectangular mass against the starry sky, with its great shadow on the white strand. Just then we entered the shadow. It was fancy, no doubt, but it seemed to me that I grew colder. We drew nigh to Dun-Randal, but still not the faintest light showed anywhere in the dark tower. The entrance faced northwards, an unusual feature, and was defended by a low porch of the same material as the pile itself, therefore at any distance was lost to view in the ebon mass which was Dun-Randal. Nothing more was said till we drew up in front of that porch.

The youth called Brian, who was not given to conversation, but who nevertheless seemed active, ready, resourceful, and obliging, now unstrapped my saddle-bags, and carried them into this porch. Conahar, who did not seem to remember my coldness, was about to lead away my horse, when, turning again quickly, he said—

"One word, sir, before we part. If you have *private* speech with the young lady, tell her that I have come back from Limerick, and that *the Baron* never sailed.

"Is that all?"

"Yes, sir; she will understand; and God keep you, sir, and send you safe out of Dun-Randal," he added, in a different tone. He looked full at me as he said it, saluted gravely, and turning away led off my tired mare across the sands. As he went, I could hear him talking to her affectionately in Gaelic, quite as if the poor beast could comprehend him. Perhaps she did.

"A singular young man," I murmured, as I

gazed after that receding pair and their moving shadows.

"A first-rate soldier," observed my now sole companion, who had overheard me, "with a great gift of speech and an understanding like few."

Entering the porch I beat strongly again and again on the main door with the butt of one of my pistols, which I had transferred from the holsters to my girdle, Brian's rappings there seeming to have elicited no response. Save echoing reverberations from the interior, though we listened attentively we could hear no other sound.

"Sir, the key is there," remarked my companion, as he stooped and peered into the lock. "Say the word, and I'll turn her fast enough. Faith, 'tis in my mind that I'm not called 'Brian of the Locks' for nothing. For Brian of the Locks O Hara is my name, and I was a locksmith before I went soldiering for Rig-Shamus" (King James), "and now I'm a locksmith again, and never a penny the richer."

Hardly waiting for a reply, he dropped that little leathern bag to which I formerly referred, whipped from it a certain steel instrument resembling a large tweezers, inserted it in the keyhole, and in a trice the door was wide open. With his little engine he had, in fact, nipped the head of the key, and turned it by main force in the lock.

"Indeed, Brian," I said, laughing, "thou art the best of picklocks. But is not this a dangerous liberty to take with any honest gentleman's door?"

"Maybe so," he answered cheerfully; "but sure your honour will bear me out in the act. And another thing, sir," he added slyly, "sunrise will see me a good twenty mile from here. God send your honour safe out of this lonesome locality."

I handed Brian a guinea, which was accepted and joyfully pouched, and never again saw Brian of the Locks O Hara. But of his road-comrade, Conahar of the Red Hair, the ready tongue, and honest-seeming countenance, I was to see a great deal. Indeed, as I write these lines, Conahar is teaching one of my grandsons how to shoot out of a piece. As Brian of the Locks disappeared into the night, stepping westwards over the sands, I crossed the echoing threshold and stood within the dark tower by the sea.

CHAPTER IV

THE LAME GIANT

I STOOD now in a spacious but gloomy chamber, the great hall of the castle. At the far end an expiring fire just lived in its ashes. Two candles and the glow of the embers barely sufficed to make the darkness visible. I raised my voice. No answer save sinister echoes from remote parts of the castle! A black cat of great size rose from the hearth, stretched himself like a dog, and slowly disappeared into darkness. In dim chiaroscuro I could see on the walls the crooked projections of stags' antlers, some dusky suits of mail, targets, pikes, and other arms, antiquities or of an antique pattern. On my right, close to the castle door, a flight of stone steps led down to the basement cellars. Listening at the head of these steps I thought I heard the echoing there of some noise at a great distance. I took one of the candles and descended, looking well to my feet as I went,

for the descent was steep. At the foot of the
flight was an open door, and beyond, darkness.
This door was of great strength. The first
sight which caught my eye, as I stood on what
was apparently the basement, was the glint of
steel. It came from a great number of matchlocks leaning against the walls. The floor
of the cellar was at a certain point crowded
with barrels containing powder, as I guessed—
" lasts," we called them in King William's army.
I noticed several huge coils of match, slow
match for firelocks, quick for firing mines.
Passing onwards I came to a very low, strong
table, to which was attached by screws a curious and complicated piece of iron mechanism.
Laying hold of a short projecting bar I found
that by turning it the whole mechanism moved,
and so freely, that it was plain that the machinery,
whatever might be its purpose, was well oiled
in all its joints, and had perhaps been recently
used. I took it to be some new-fashioned warlike engine.

While with the inquisitiveness of a soldier
I puzzled for some time over this curious bit
of iron work, I heard a door slam-to with a
metallic clash, awaking strange echoes through

this great subterranean chamber, and almost immediately afterwards a sudden and furious Irish imprecation. Presently a gigantic figure, bearing a lanthorn, came rushing swiftly towards me. From the jerking motion of the lanthorn I perceived that the angry person who bore it was lame. As he came, he continued to roar Gaelic curses, oaths, and passionate interrogations. I laid my candle on a barrel-head, and standing behind it, drew my sword and one of my *bombardules*. I could see something flashing in the vicinity of that lanthorn, no doubt steel.

"Halt, fellow," I cried ; "not another step, as you value your life."

I had him covered with my pistol as I spoke. He came to a sudden stand a few paces before me, his face and form showing clear against the darkness. The face at its best could never have been an agreeable one, and now, pale and disturbed by passion, was quite hideous. He was a middle-aged man, inclined to elderly, with well-grizzled hair, and a countenance wrinkled and rugged beyond description. His small eyes glittered under bristling brows. His face, flat and abnormally developed in the

lower parts, seemed to promise a minimum of
intelligence and a maximum of stern, perhaps
brutal, resolution ; and his great stature and the
breadth of his shoulders, extraordinary physical
strength.   Seeing the fury depicted in his face,
mingled with what I thought to be alarm and
the sense of having been overfallen and surprised, I rejoiced that I had descended into
these cellars armed with something besides my
sword.   In his left hand he carried a basket,
within which lay a coil of rope.

Suddenly the expression of his features
changed to one of obsequiousness, but the
smile which accompanied the change was
hardly less pleasing than that former murderous
look.   He flung his sword aside.   It was evidently one which he had snatched up in this
underground armoury as he rushed towards
me, for he wore no belt and hanger.

"Surely," he said in English, "your honour
is the young gentleman, the master's cousin,
that we were expecting.   Sir, have a care with
your candle, for there's a power of powder
about here.   But the old master and the young
masters are abroad, and the Lady Sheela is
on the say (sea) ; and a quare young lady she

is, to be spending her days and nights on the salt water. It passes me to tell how your honour came in," he added, looking at me with a wild suspicion.

"Through the door, man. How else?" I replied.

This seemed to puzzle him, but he only said—

"Step up, sir. Sure, there must be hunger upon you."

As I ascended to the great hall I heard him muttering behind me while he locked the cellar door. Reaching the great hall he went straight to the castle door, which he held in both his hands, swaying it a little to and fro while he seemed to ruminate. Enjoying the puzzled condition of the fellow's mind, I took a seat by the fire and expanded my hands to the feeble glow.

"I was certain sure I locked it," I heard him mutter—a remark, however, to which I made no reply.

"Come to the withdrawing-room, sir," he added, "you'll find things *tastier* there."

I followed him to the next floor, and into small room, which was furnished with muc elegance, according to the standard of that period. There were soft chairs and lounges; the walls were draperied with a hanging arras, brilliantly embroidered; the floor was richly carpeted. A bright fire of turf and bog-wood shed a cheerful light through the room, and in the light various ornaments of the precious metals and of glass or crystal made faint coruscations. The lame man departed, and presently returned with a bottle of wine and a loaf of bread.

"There will be supper," he said, "when the gentlemen come back; but I'm thinking your honour won't find this amiss after your ride."

He now, though his remarks in the cellar seemed to promise garrulity, resisted my attempts to draw him into conversation. In short, I perceived that he was naturally a silent, perhaps misanthropic, sort of man, but probably, and perhaps owing to that very reason, an excellent servant. So far as I could see, all the servant work of the establishment was done by him.

Evidently my last letter, that in which I announced the day of my arrival, had not come into Sir Theodore's hands. At all events, no preparations had been made for my recep-

tion.   While I ate and drank, I could hear the
man busy overhead getting my room into
order, and disposing there the contents of my
saddle-bags.   Things now began to assume a
rosier complexion.   I was warm ; the pangs of
hunger had been allayed; the light but generous
wine disposed my mind to a more cheerful view
of the situation ; and youth, hope, and a very
ardent temperament did the rest.   I fell to thinking about the Lady Sheela, the "young lady
who spent her days and nights on the salt
water," and for whom the youth called Conahar
had charged me with that mysterious message.
I had not heard of her before.   To any young
man of twenty-three no young woman is un-
interesting.   So my thoughts not unnaturally
began to revolve round that young lady.   Was
she tall and stately, or petite and winsome,
proud or humble, dark or fair, wild or civilised ?
Wild, I rather feared—wild, shy, and unsophisticated.   What else could she be, dwelling in
this wilderness, probably reared here ?   Nor, I
said to myself, shall I be surprised to find her
a prey to the vast melancholia which seems
to be the one fixed feature of this lonely and
savage region.   Sheela was a pretty name

nevertheless—Gaelic for Julia—and, hoyden as
no doubt I would find her, she might supply
conversation and society agreeable as a change
should I tire of my martial, but possibly un-
interesting, male cousins.

In the light of such thoughts, supplemented,
I confess, by that moderate supply of Ceres and
Bacchus, things generally looked brighter, and
I found myself smiling at the former sinister
cast of my reflections. Castles exposed to the
briny winds of the sea, and never touched by
the limer, could not be brilliant. Wild sunsets
were not so uncommon. A drab-coloured
castle seen clear against such a sunset would
naturally look black. What other hue *could*
it present? A daft woman is found in every
country side. Why should a sane man attach
any importance to the ravings of such? A
family quarrel or feud would account for
Conahar's malignant representations. The lame
man was a tough, hard, ill-favoured old fellow
to be sure; but what of that? Old faithful re-
tainers do develop curious traits and manners,
and the man was quite right to be alarmed and
angry at the sight of an unbidden visitor, candle
in hand, in the midst of a powder magazine.

Nor was I much surprised to find my cousin the possessor of such a warlike store. It was only a few months since the last shot had been fired in our war. Probably such stores lay in the basement cellars of a good many Jacobite gentlemen's castles besides that of Sir Theodore. The basket and coil of rope? Well, I could not explain everything. All this time I heard the man moving about over my head, stamping heavily with the lame leg and lightly with the sound one. From without came the long roar of the waves upon the sand and the deeper boom of the billows breaking against an iron coast, also at intervals the wild cries of those little sand-birds, the nightingales of the Atlantic sea-board.

And now for the first time, piercing, shrill, and terrible, rang the cry of that poor desolate creature, that watcher by the quicksands, long-sustained, toned to an unutterable anguish. That terrible cry went through me like a sword. All my misgivings, my dim alarms and apprehensions started up anew, and with a treble power to agitate and disturb. "And I," I said, as I sprang to my feet, "am I not in the castle, in the power of the men who have caused that anguish, in the castle of the Great Dhoul?"

CHAPTER V

THE LADY SHEELA

I SPRANG, I say, to my feet. The next moment I heard a quick, light step and the rustle of female garments. Some one stood motionless in the dark doorway. A woman ? Yes and no ; say rather the star which I had seen shining above the black battlements of Dun-Randal transformed into flesh and blood.

God, being Almighty, may have created, but surely God never did create a human countenance like that which now, still as a picture, yet charged nevertheless with some intense life and meaning, gazed at me from the darkness ! A young girl, tall, yet in years seemingly little more than a child, stood there, clad in a mantle of dark blue clasped with silver, the hood thrown back, over which rolled in confusion a torrent of auburn hair. Her complexion was of dazzling brilliancy, white and ruddy, her large eyes full and

glowing with a certain steady fire, the whole
expression frank, daring, proud, almost uncon-
querable—and still that fixed, earnest, searching gaze. Never for an instant remitting that
strange look, she crossed the floor towards me
with a swift motion and elastic step, reaching
forth a gloved hand as she came.

"You are Sir Theodore's cousin?" she said.
Her voice, though low-toned and feminine,
rang clear and true as a silver bell, tuned to
an exquisite modulation, with something foreign
in the tone of it. She took my hand in hers,
and held it. Still that searching look. "I—believed—surely—that——" The last words came
slowly from her parted and hardly moving lips.
Of my embarrassment, which must have been
evident, she appeared to be quite unconscious.

Then suddenly she released my hand and
cried—"Hugh Netterville, you are not one of
them. You are a *man*. Why are you here?"

While I endeavoured to explain, she interrupted me.

"Nay, not so many words. Time presses.
They will be here anon. Take a young girl's
counsel who would be your friend. Fly now,
and at once. The great lame man may with-

stand you. Run him through with your sword.
Have no pity ; they will have none. Escape
to the hills, anywhere, only put as great a distance as the night will permit between you and
this den of demons. Trust me. Do I look like
one who would deceive ? "

"Hark ! " she cried, raised a hand, and
listened.

I heard far away the note of a bugle.

"They are leaving the village," she said.
"There is yet time if you go as with wings."

I was amazed, astounded, struck for a moment
dumb. "Surely, surely," I said, "I have never
seen awake or in vision a face like yours to
awaken trust and love. As God is my witness,
that is true. Yet who is not liable to error ?
These gentlemen are my kindred, my nearest
on earth. They are of an ancient and honourable house, approved soldiers, who fought for
the King of their choice, as I for mine. They
invite me to their castle, where, without once
seeing their faces, I murder their servant, and
fly. To act so were against religion, honour,
and reason. Moreover," I said, something kindling in me as I said so, "it is not customary with
me to fly danger."

She did not seem to hear or heed me, only again raised her hand and said, " Hark ! "

Now I heard faintly a chorus of men's voices indistinctly singing.

" It is your kindred and their bloody men. Oh for darkness and storm—for the strand lies white under the moon.   And yet there is time, but in a moment it will be too late.   One word then, do you go or stay ? "

" Then God help me, sweet lady," I said, " for I stay."

If the devil himself were due at Dun-Randal that night I would have stayed.   Love the Hunter suddenly and unawares had taken me in his golden toils.

Her hands fell to her side.   Her whole form, face, hair, pose of head, till this moment charged and instinct with a fiery energy, showed such a change, as if some interior flame had suddenly been extinguished.

" Yet if what you say is true," I added, " you too are in peril.   Why are *you* here ?   Why do *you* stay ? "

This I said with a smile.

" I am a prisoner," she said ; " also, I stay with a purpose."

"And who art thou thyself, lady? Of my west-country cousins I never heard of any save Sir Theodore and his three sons, Enoch, Israel, and Immanuel."

"I am the Lady Sheela de Stanton, sister of Raymond the Baron, who, as they give out, has sailed for Spain."

"He never sailed," I said, remembering the charge of the young soldier.

"Who bade you say that?"

"A very young man, a soldier, of a free and bold bearing, ruddy-haired, and of a florid complexion. He called himself Conahar."

"Yes, my foster-brother, Conahar MacArdell, and he sends me word of what I know, travelled a hundred miles to learn—nothing. For asleep or awake I have *seen* my dear brother, my dear, dear brother, dungeoned, in irons, and knew that he was in *their* power—somewhere, somewhere."

Her beautiful eyes filled with tears, and her voice trembled. I heard now, still far away, the strains of *Lillibulero* sung boisterously in wild chorus. It was a favourite Jacobite air before we Williamites took it up and made it our own, adding new words.

"Did Conahar tell you aught else?" she asked.

"Nay, I did not permit him. He reviled my kinsmen, and I would not hearken."

Her manner again changed. She looked at me not unkindly, but with a certain light mockery.

"You are good and brave," she said, "but guileless—oh, so guileless."

For a moment she seemed to reflect, then swiftly removed her gloves, sank on her knees at my side, and drew from some inner pocket in her raiment a folding of fine leather. While I wondered what all this might mean, she had in a trice cut with scissors a little incision in the lining of my long-skirted waistcoat. Between lining and minever she placed something which I could not see, and from the same repertory drawing a needle and thread, sewed up the little rent.

While she wrought, I was conscious of a faint, sweet odour which exhaled from her whole person.

So humble was the posture, so full of gentle feminine serviceableness and humility the action, that I found it difficult to believe that this was the same girl who a moment before had gazed at me with those bold, searching eyes, and given that murderous counsel.

Then she sprang to her feet, and made me a low, even coquettish, curtsey, with something in it of mock humility.

So nimbly had wrought her swift fingers, that it was all done in less time than I have taken to record the action.

"And this little gift, Lady Sheela," I said inquiringly, indeed playfully, as to some capricious, unreasonable, and self-willed child, "is it a talisman or charm, or what?"

"Sir Untrustful Proud, thou mayest find a humble but good ally in this little gift when thy pride and self-confidence are brought down to the dust. It is only a little fishing-line, with a little glandule of lead for sinker. Some time you may find yourself fishing with it—for your life."

This was said mockingly. Then with a return to her former earnest manner, she added—

"Seem to suspect nothing; observe all things. Unless you are duller than a—than a *clam*, you will soon learn why you are here."

The next moment I was alone, and it

seemed to me that the room perceptibly darkened. Nay, it did darken.

I heard now from without, seemingly at the
castle door, boisterous and ill-sung, and as if
rendered by a chorus of tipsy rioters, the
familiar strains of *Lillibulero—bullen-a-la*. There
was a company entering the castle, arrived, as
I had no doubt, from that village lying at the
tip of the sandy tongue.

While Sheela was with me my whole soul had
been possessed by her radiant beauty. Now
other thoughts and emotions came surging up
in my mind. The young girl's counsel that I
should escape from Dun-Randal on the instant,
even at the cost of murder, was but the climax of
an ascending scale of omens and ominous com-
munications which had been accompanying me
all day long, even from the early dawn. Nor
was there anything reassuring, but much the reverse, in the tipsy roaring of this Jacobite horde
which was now invading the castle, and spread-
ing like a tumultuous flood through the lower
regions, whence arose a loud clinking of cups
and cans, and the noise of boisterous pledg-
ings. And here was I, a solitary Williamite,
with nothing to trust in save the honour and

cousinly feeling of unknown kinsmen. Needless to say, I now longed to stand as soon as possible face to face with these men, concerning whom I had heard such things said and such things suggested, and learn what they were from one look in their eyes. I had some notion that I could distinguish honest men and rogues at sight.

Then, after what seemed an interminably long time, I heard the clamour of loud farewells discharged into the night, and responded to from the night, and again *Lillibulero* receding, dying away in the distance. That was to me a welcome sound. Those who departed were a great company. The silence which now reigned below seemed to indicate that none had remained behind. It was not so, for presently I heard beneath me low voices of uncertain import, the great lame man's being one of them.

"Seem to suspect nothing; observe all things;" such were my instructions.

That would seem to debar the possibility of immediate violence. Nevertheless, I loosened my sword in the sheath, looked at and replaced my pistols in my belt, and generally braced

D

myself and hardened my heart. I was not in the least afraid; on the contrary, felt rather elated. The near approach of danger does, I think, always produce a sort of joy in the heart of man, a mysterious organ at whose singular and not to be predicted motions and workings I have often wondered.

Now on the castle stairs I heard quick ascending footsteps. Something like the *dénouement* of a drama was about to unfold, for the approaching steps were almost certainly those of my cousin Sir Theodore. I was about to meet face to face that man, the mention of whose name had changed to granite the countenance of my innkeeper in the early morning, concerning whom Conahar and the Lady Sheela had said or intimated such dreadful things, who seemed to be the genius of this desolate and melancholy region, lord of this black sinister castle, and whom the poor insane girl on the sands had called the Great Dhoul. He and I were now to meet.

CHAPTER VI

THE GREAT DHOUL

NATURALLY I expected at least to meet in my cousin a person of strong and commanding individuality, capable of attracting hatred, of exciting suspicion, and becoming the object of general alarm and dread—good or evil, an alarming kind of man. Judge, then, of my surprise when a little elderly gentleman stepped briskly into the room, and hastening forward with outstretched hands, greeted me with the utmost cordiality and goodwill; neat, nay elegant, in his attire, and of an address most frank, engaging, and very well-bred, evidently one who had mixed much in the most courtly society, yet without losing in such intercourse those simple, natural virtues which are so ill replaced by mere brilliancy and polish of manner. There followed him a very tall and singularly, even strikingly, handsome young man, with a bright and engaging smile, whom he introduced to me as "Enoch, my eldest, heir to nothing and my sword."

Sir Theodore wore a full-bottomed peruke and snow-white bands, and at his wrists the finest lace. His hands, in time's despite, were long, white, and almost as elegantly shaped as a lady's; yet they closed upon mine with a strong and masculine grasp. He wore several rings. I shall not weary the reader with a detailed description of his costume, the more so as he seldom wore the same raiment twice. Suffice it to say that, to my eyes, as yet unfamiliar with courts, and whose acquaintances, when not soldiers, had been the plain rural gentry of my province, Sir Theodore's dress was not only rich but splendid, and no doubt in the topmost height of the fashion as practised at Paris and St. Germains. In any other man of his years the effect might have been displeasing; but his vivid and animated countenance, the litheness and vivacity of his movements, and the sparkle and vivacity of his manner and conversation, seemed to demand some such sumptuosity and glitter of attire. Of the character and contour of his features, I have not even now a clear remembrance. I believe they were homely, rather than handsome. I remember distinctly only a florid countenance, the brilliancy of grey-blue eyes, the ceaseless play of expression around his lips, a pronounced chin, and a long jaw, which is said to be a sign of wit. Indeed, I believe that his features were decidedly what might be called irregular. But the play of expression there was so ceaseless, that it would need a very cold-blooded observer to describe them one by one— and I was by no means cold-blooded. As to temperament, he was decidedly mercurial. I may mention that a jewelled snuff-box was seldom out of his hands, which he tapped continually.

My cousin Enoch, his eldest son, was about my own height, that is to say, somewhat over six feet, but was, I should say, far more gracefully proportioned than myself, for as to figure, I believe I could only boast a powerful and athletic frame, developed from childhood by field-sports and other manly pastimes, and latterly by the exercises of war. Unlike his father, Enoch wore his own hair, which was coal-black, and long and curling at the ends. His attire was lace and velvet. His face was long and olive-complexioned, and his eyes large and dark, not full of slumbrous fire as is common in such eyes, but glittering, a feature which struck me, like the dark eyes of Oriental races.   His motions were singularly graceful, his manners quiet and gracious.   Altogether, he looked like a young gallant of the Elizabethan times clad in the costume of those of the Second Charles.   His voice, with a foreign accent in its tones, was low, modulated, and almost caressing.   In short, I admired and liked in the extreme both father and son, diverse as they were.   In one moment all those vain alarms and suspicions vanished from my mind, like bats and night-birds at the coming of day.   I remember distinctly, for I had little personal, though much family pride, how pleased I was to think that my nearest surviving kinsmen were so evidently gentlemen, who in any assembly of the brilliant and the great might more fitly be tempted to apologise for me than I for them.   The Barretts, though, as I had reason to believe, very poor, had plainly in many important respects the advantage of myself, though I represented the apparently wealthier and more prosperous line of the Nettervilles.   Then beneath their polished manners they were obviously full of plain, unsophisticated good-nature and cousinly feeling. Nothing could exceed the cordiality and frankness with which they welcomed me "to Dun-Randal." Whether due to professional soldiering, or to whatever other occupation or employment which they had pursued abroad in the course of their roving life, my kinsfolk, though landless, as I knew them to be, were plainly in anything but indigent circumstances. A man who thinks that he is being led to the scaffold, though with some wild hope of springing from the cart, and of fighting his way to freedom, and who suddenly, unbandaged, finds himself in the midst of merry and laughing friends, may feel some such emotions as were mine on the entrance of Sir Theodore and Enoch ; and this sense of relief on my part, nay, of joyful satisfaction, was deepened by every turn in their manner and conversation. Enoch's somewhat Spanish, I might almost say Iberno-Spanish, dignity and gravity of behaviour, not at all without a corresponding sweetness and urbanity, contrasted pleasantly with the gaiety and bright conversational effervescence of his father.

As to manner, indeed, Sir Theodore was just a little more pronounced, more caressing, than was quite customary amongst us plain home-bred Irish gentlemen. This, however, was natural, and to be expected in one who had passed so much of his life abroad, for the most part in France. Presently Enoch, expressing many cordial and cousinly sentiments, took a courteous leave, no doubt with the object of leaving his father and me alone.

Sir Theodore won still more upon my regard now by his conversation about my parents, for both of whom he seemed to entertain a singular affection and respect. He spoke much of my father, and related some merry tales of their school-days, for they had been at school together. "Your mother," he said, "never, I think, quite forgave me for calling my sons by such very pronounced Scriptural names. Indeed, to be quite frank, the boys had a very wealthy aunt, of a devout temper, and it occurred to me that I might put them in the way of good-fortune in that quarter, seeing that I could do so little for them myself. But it all came to nothing," he added pleasantly.

"Indeed, I believe your father succeeded to the bulk of my Aunt Onora's property."

Seeing me a little disconcerted at this family reminiscence, he laid his hand on my arm, and said kindly—

"But I am glad of that, dear cousin. It might have all wandered away to religious, or charitable purposes, and been quite lost."

I did not quite see the logic of this, so volunteered no remark.

He then inquired in the kindest manner into my affairs, concerning which as between near relatives I spoke very freely, informing him that in view of the profession which I had adopted, and with a view to forwarding my interests therein, I had converted nearly the whole of my landed estates into cash. At this point I had the temerity to tell him of the cousinly tribute of goodwill and affection which I had brought with me. I was about to unbuckle my treasure-belt and lay it wholly in his hands, when he gently but decisively restrained me. He was, however, so much affected by this proof of my regard, that he was forced to turn aside in order to hide his emotion. Needless to say, I did not further invade this very

honourable and creditable pride of my kinsman.

After this somewhat awkward incident he
resumed the conversation in a lighter tone, and
enlarged a little on his family history.

" For forty miles round," he said, " all this
country was once Barrett property. Yet of it
I inherit nothing save this dismal keep, like a
rock in a world submerged. This, right or
wrong, I determined to retain as a *point d'appui*,
whence under altered circumstances I might
reassert inherent and indestructible rights.
From these walls my father beat back a party
of Ireton's people."

He crossed himself when he mentioned his
father's name, and murmured something which
I could not hear.

" I don't think you ever met him," he resumed. " He was a great man, my father ;
feared neither——" He was silent, and gazed
before him with a look which my neighbours
in the province of Ulster would call *raised*.
" Well, well," he went on, " Dun-Randal for
good or evil I resolved to keep in my own
hands. Going abroad, I left here as constable
a very faithful servitor, who is with me still,

the great lame man whom, doubtless, you have met. Had the rightful King won" (this with a smile at our dynastical differences)—"well, well, coz, you and your friends are in the sun now."

A wild glare of some to me utterly untranslatable expression swept again for a single instant across his face. It might have sprung from the bitter reflection that now as an old man he was about to repeat anew in age the experiences of a wandering and exiled youth.

In the ensuing pause I remarked upon the number of soldiers still in his service.

"Yes," he said, "my years notwithstanding, I am off soldiering again, this time with the Spanish king, if he will have me. If not, I can present him with three good sons and some 200 soldiers, who only want a little drilling and disciplining to be first-rate men of war. We await almost daily the arrival of our transport."

"Some ten miles eastward," said I, laughing as I recalled the experience, "on my way hither I was challenged by two most unpromising-looking rascals." I gave my cousin a humorous description of that adventure with the rapparees in the glen, at which he was good enough to laugh heartily.

"But you must remember, cousin," he said, "that the best soldiers will get out of hand under relaxed discipline ; and if I will not humour those fellows and give them their own way a little, I shall never be able to embark them for the Groyne. The ship which I have chartered for that purpose will be here anon. It is the same in which my young neighbour, Raymond de Stanton, and some young bloods of his acquaintance, sailed for Spain not long since."

"I have not seen the name of the Baron de Stanton," I said, "in the list of the gentlemen who have gone abroad since the cessation of the civil wars."

"Very likely," he replied. "There was some difficulty with the Governor of Galway, which compelled him to sail incognito. I may add, too, that his title of Baron is only one of courtesy. On this side of the Shannon the head of the de Stantons is always Baron. His sister, the Lady Sheela de Stanton, a singularly beautiful girl, is here now, and under my protection, a protection which, though meant for her good, I think she somewhat resents."

Sailed incognito ! What a complete mare's nest then was Conahar's supposed discovery !

"Indeed," he went on to say, "I am here on his business, not my own ; for my unlucky house, as I have already told you, has, through ill fortune and our own deserts, lost all connection with the county. Raymond de Stanton, with whom my sons were very intimate during the last few months of the war, commissioned me to collect all arrears of rent on his estates (I have his authority signed and sealed to that effect), and to follow him with the same, also with some treasure and valuables left in his own house hard by, not a bow-shot from where we sit."

"You mean," I interjected, "the low square house westward, which looks like the last of a chain of castles."

"Precisely. Raymond de Stanton and his sister, orphans, resided there till the boy took sword and came to Limerick to fight for *the King*. I am a Jacobite, Cousin Hugh, and must speak as such. For some years the estate, which is a very large one, has been

controlled by the lad himself, with the con-
sent, I believe, of his guardian, Sir Nicholas
Bingham, slain in the battle of Aughrim.   The
boy, I presume, has no legal right to appoint
any one to collect his rents, he being still a
minor ; but in these unsettled times, when
legality is nothing, the young Baron's written
directions are authority enough for me.   You
won't bring the Governor and his army down
on me for that irregularity, I hope, cousin ?"

I only laughed.

" Have you had success in this rent-collect-
ing business ?" I asked.   " To me, fresh from
the rich plains of Meath, it seems a region
which might yield sport indeed, but, full surely,
little in the way of profit."

" There is your mistake, cousin.   Between
the bogs and mountains there is much rich
land which does not meet the eye.   Nay, land
which seems barren is often very fattening for
sheep.   Moreover, the young Baron allowed
the rents to run unconscionably during the
term of his control.   The money due as rent
by his tenants and free-holders was there, but
in concealed hoards ; our only difficulty has
been in compelling the roguish peasants and

dishonest minor gentry to disgorge. Some
were for driving their cattle and chattels across
the mearings, but we stopped that by planting
soldiers in all the outgates of Stanton-land.
It was two such whom you frightened this
morning."

"The name of this castle," I said, "is somewhat singular, Dun-Randal on the Sea."

"That is to distinguish it from yon tree-girt
house, now Baronscourt, but known also in
former days as Dun-Randal. The de Stantons
and Barretts were for many generations at feud.
We were worsted, both in war and in the law
courts; and it is, I believe, a very ancient
maxim that the loser pays."

Again that *raised* look. It was gone in a
moment, and yet it puzzled me.

CHAPTER VII

ENOCH, ISRAEL, AND IMMANUEL

WHILE I listened to and looked at my cousin, I could hardly forbear a smile as I recalled that singularly inappropriate and even ludicrously inapplicable title, "the Great Dhoul," as applied to Sir Theodore even by a poor demented creature. Neither in mind nor in body did he show any trait or quality in the least suggestive of a sobriquet so ominous. He talked ceaselessly, and with a smile. Indeed, his frankness tended somewhat to garrulity. I, on my side, was equally frank. I revealed to him all my hopes and purposes, to the details of which he listened with the kindest attention, and gave me much useful advice with regard to foreign military service.

Enoch now returned, bringing with him his two brothers, Israel and Immanuel, both tall, swarthy, and handsome; both richly dressed in lace and velvet, and resembling himself, with a difference. The youngest, Immanuel, I observed with regret, was somewhat the worse for liquor. On being introduced, he stared at me in a disconcerting manner. His brothers, however, contrived to suppress him. Perceiving that he might be troublesome, they succeeded in getting him to a seat in the wide hearthplace, where from time to time I was aware that his great black eyes were directed towards me. Israel was stouter in body, and shorter in face than his eldest brother, who was tall and slender, and of a very aquiline countenance. If Israel were the Lothario of the family, as the wild words of that poor mad creature would seem to suggest, he did not look the character, for, in repose, the expression of his face was sombre. Like Enoch's, his manner towards myself was both courteous and kind. It was somewhat amusing to think that Sir Theodore, small, dainty, gay, fair, and debonair, was the father of three such great, swarthy, and handsome sons. The attire of all four, even of Immanuel, was unusually handsome and rich.

Such attention to dress in such a dismal and savage place, and such success of achievement,

E

considering the poor nature of the accommo-
dation and the apparent absence of attendance,
were very singular.

As supper-time was now approaching, Sir
Theodore conducted me himself to my sleeping apartment, and was as attentive as possible,
in his own way, chatting ceaselessly all the
time.   He reminded me that my pistols would
suffer from the damp of a fireless chamber ;
and calling aloud for the lame man, whom
he called " Fergananim," bade him keep them
in a dry place.   Having seen personally to
my wants, he skipped away, while I wondered
at the boyish animation and alacrity of his
movements, and laughed at the idea of the
Evil Principle assuming such a form as that
of this cheery, agreeable, lively, and amiable
old knight.

To me now it was quite plain that, be the
cause what it might, Lady Sheela de Stanton
was the victim of some wild, irrational suspicions.   The face and form of this fair girl
had been hardly for a moment absent from
my mind ever since she left me.   I feared
to ask Sir Theodore any question concerning
her, believing that I could not do so without

revealing the state of my mind towards her.
Was I ever to see her again ? Her manner
and words at parting seemed to suggest that that
was to be our last interview. There was much
that was quite unaccountable in her position
here. Curious questions, which I could not
solve, concerning her rose perpetually in my
mind. Trusting that the events and conversation of the evening would prove the solu-
tion of these, and thinking of many things
not easy now to particularise or write down,
though their drift may be imagined, I dressed
myself and descended.

At the same time I felt surprised, nay, even
enraged, with myself at the facility with which
I had listened to the most abominable charges
urged against my own nearest relations. Was
it not my clear duty, I reflected, to acquaint Sir
Theodore and his sons with those calumnies ?
My position was growing every moment more
intolerable. I was Sir Theodore's guest as
well as his kinsman, the partaker of his hospitality, treated by him and his sons with the
utmost kindness and cousinly goodwill ; yet
was I not also the confidant and in some
sense the secret ally and confederate of one

who had brought against him the terrible accusations which I in a weak moment had so far entertained as not to repel and contradict with natural and proper indignation ? Had I not too virtually undertaken to play here the vile part of a spy. " Seem to suspect nothing ; observe all things," were Sheela's last instructions, and by my silence I had virtually promised action in consonance with those instructions. And yet ever and anon, while the blood burned in my cheeks at the remembrance of these things, the pure, clear, childlike face of Sheela de Stanton—childlike for all its imperiousness—and the earnest eyes with such sorrow and trouble in their depths, would rise before my imagination and compel all my thoughts and emotions to return into that channel in which they flowed when she was by my side and while I was still under the glamour of her pure, fresh beauty. In short, I was profoundly distressed and embarrassed. I desired with my whole soul to bear myself through these strange complications in a manner worthy of a gentleman and a man of honour, but felt very uncertain indeed in which direction for me the path of honour lay. Possibly but for the personal feelings with which I regarded my child-ally, and which were in fact dawning and nascent love, I might have revealed everything to my host during our *tête-à-tête* conversation, so degrading and dishonourable did my position appear in my eyes.

As I descended the narrow stairs, my cousins seemed to be engaged in a fraternal *mêlée*—not by any means a bad symptom, for quarrelling and rough mutual usage are perhaps really a better sign of family affection than cold politeness. Passing an unglazed slit or shot-vent in the wall my candle went out, and finding myself in utter darkness, I had to grope my way down slowly. My light house-shoes and the sound of their own voices prevented my approach from being heard.

" Get what he has and don't bother," I heard Immanuel say in his thick, tipsy voice. " You fellows, when you catch a soft one, are like a cat with a mouse. The m-m-mouse is no bigger in the end."

" Thou'rt a drunken blockhead," cried Israel. "If he's for women now, one of my cast-asides——"

" Drop all that," shouted Sir Theodore, in a
high, clangorous voice ; " let us talk of your
cousin." Here he began to use some words
concerning myself too complimentary to be set
down, and which I interrupted by laughingly
declaring the nature of my situation, and beg-
ging for a light.

Sir Theodore himself furnished the necessary illumination. He was assisted by Enoch
and Israel, and the three conducted me hilari-
ously into the withdrawing-room, where Immanuel still sat in the chimney-nook with a
broken clay pipe at his feet, but never offered
to stir as I entered the room.

Of whom the brothers had been talking
when Sir Theodore directed the conversation
to myself, saying things—I may as well be a
little specific — which were peculiarly welcome to a lover's ear, things that he said
" Sheela " had confessed to him, I did not
know and did not care. Israel, then, was a
Lothario, and a shameless one ; but what was
that to me. I had known many such even in
our own army. I was sorry, nevertheless.

Sir Theodore on my entrance resumed the
conversation, and talked continuously. In-

deed, I began to discover that his talk tended
to garrulity and tedious anecdotage, so much
so, that in spite of the very respectful and
attentive demeanour of his sons, it occurred
to me that he might be a mere cypher amongst
those great dark and eagle-nosed men. But I
judged like a simpleton. Immanuel, as I have
mentioned, sat in the wide hearth-place, where
he presently filled and lit another long pipe.
He sat on the outer end of one of the benches
which flanked the fire. So some, but not
all, of the offensive vapour escaped by the
chimney.

"Get you further in, sir ; further."

This order came from Sir Theodore in a
tone that reminded me of the crack of a whip.
I started a little, so utterly unexpected was
this exhibition of energy and authority. I
looked at Sir Theodore, but he was smiling as
gaily as before, getting lightly forward with
a trivial anecdote, which was concerned, as
I remember, with a certain "Sir Toby Butler,"
and some witty reply made by him to the
Duchess of Tyrconnell. It was plain to me
that a man who could speak like that must
be the master here.

CHAPTER VIII

LOVE'S MIGHT AND POWER

PRESENTLY Sir Theodore, regarding me with
more of gravity and directness than he had
hitherto used, left the room, but almost immediately returned.   Resuming his seat, he
continued to glance from time to time at
the door with an expression of impatience.
He was certainly expecting some one.   Could
it be Sheela ?   My heart beat faster at the
thought.   Then I heard descending steps—
slow, halting, and hesitating, also the rustle
of female garments.   A face appeared in the
dark doorway.   It was Sheela's, but I did
not at first recognise her.   All the colour
had fled from her cheeks.   Her face was
white, her eyes scared.   Owing to my position I alone could see her, and, just at that
moment, something said or done by Immanuel had attracted the attention of the
rest.   When her eyes met mine her whole

expression changed to one of pleasure, which
in turn gave place to a look of the gravest
warning, which she emphasized with a raised
hand.   I could interpret the look very well.
It meant "remember" and "take heed."

She entered the room with a firm step and
a certain stateliness, nay, pride, something even
of defiance in her air and the pose of her head.
She hardly acknowledged the courtly bows
of my cousins, but turned and looked towards
me, as if awaiting an introduction.   Her kirtle
was a dark green, close-fitting, which showed
well her lithe and perfect form.   Round her
neck she wore something white, fastened with
a silver brooch.   Her kirtle was shorter, I remember, than was customary with young
girls of her age (doubtless she had outgrown
it), and the brown tongues of her silver-buckled
shoes ran far up the white instep.   Singular how I remember such things through the
mists of so many oblivious years!   Ah me!
Ah me!

Her luxuriant hair, wind-tossed and confused when last we met, was now smooth and
shining ; her face, which glowed and flushed
then, reflecting every emotion, was pale now,

pale and pure as a lily on one of my own beautiful Meathian lakes, subdued to a settled stillness and quiet, and oh! so beautiful! so transparently clear and pure. All my soul went out to her in love and worship. I bowed low in response to her grave and formal curtsey, but in spirit bowed down to the very ground. How for one moment could I have doubted such a countenance? Hysteria? No, incredible. And yet if what she said was true, what were these sombre-looking, handsome cousins? What was Sir Theodore? No doubt she had been herself deceived. Doubtless her foster-brother, for all his honest looks and frank, soldierly bearing, had abused the confidence which she reposed in him. Surely her suspicions concerning my kinsmen originated in some great error and misapprehension, which time would detect, or some sinister, groundless accusations, which as surely time would unmask. And yet, was this the face of one who could lightly entertain, could even for one moment harbour, unworthy or groundless suspicions against any human soul? Her curtseying was the most childlike feature in her behaviour that I had yet observed. It was done with a young girl's air of practising in public what she had been taught in private, neither very graceful nor very gracious, and yet under the circumstances very pretty and natural. And it was all acting—and for *me*. She took a seat near me, and I, who could never endure girls of that age and uncertain position, fresh from the hands of teachers and instructresses, bowed down in spirit before this child. Truly Love is the wind that bloweth where it listeth. We look for its advent from the north and lo ! it blows from the south, from the east, yet it cometh from the west.

Sir Theodore and his sons talked together now, seemingly with the courteous desire of permitting me some uninterrupted conversation with the only lady in our small company. Once, slightly turning her head so as not to be observed, she again gave me that warning look. All that outward calm and serenity were, then, a mask, behind which stood a spirit, alert, straining, armed, and on the watch. What was her terror ? What did she fear for me ?

Again, as before, vague alarms and appre-

hensions came over me. I looked at my
cousins, at "the Great Dhoul." He was, at
that moment, smiling apparently at nothing
at all, a faint simper just playing around his
lips. Israel was whispering some waggish incident to Enoch, something, I fancy, that had
reference to a woman. The whispering struck
me as not very well-bred. Immanuel, deep-
sunk in the chimney-nook, was nodding over
the fire, pipe in hand. I turned again to
Sheela with a look of inquiry, but her face
was a mask.

The lame giant now announced supper,
which was served in the great hall below.
Sir Theodore, with a great deal of manner
and old-fashioned, or foreign-fashioned, airs
and graces, conducted Lady Sheela by the
hand to the door. I saw her shudder when
he approached. It was indeed barely perceptible, yet my lover's eyes could not be
deceived. We descended the narrow, wind-
ing, and quite dark flight of bare stone stairs
one by one, Sir Theodore leading, and followed by Sheela. He chatted gaily as he
went; but his words fell, for me, on unconscious ears, sounding like noises in a dream.

Then in the darkness I felt something touch me.
The next moment Sheela's hand was in mine;
it trembled. I thought at first that she feared
a fall; and, indeed, unaccustomed as I was to
such tortuous flights of very narrow and slippery
stone stairs, I was at that moment paying parti-
cular attention to my own steps lest I should
stumble. But the fear which drove Sheela to
clasp my hand, nay, to search for it in the darkness, was something far different from what
at the time I had surmised it to be. Whether
the victim of hallucinations, vain apprehensions, and baseless slanders or not, fear, reaching even to the degree of terror, had prompted
this instinctive and unexpected action upon her
part. To me it was sufficiently evident that
she fled, as it were, to me for shelter and protection, like a bird chased by hawks. And
would I not protect? Ay, God helping, to
the last breath, to the last drop of my blood.
As we slowly descended, the brass-bound shoe
of my scabbard rang upon the stone stairs. I
was glad of that, for I knew that she found
a meaning in the music—felt that in the wide
world there was at least one sword that would
start with a cry from its sheath to defend her,

or to avenge. And truly, if my head was none of the wisest or most subtile, I had in those days a heart which, for war purposes, was as sound as most men's, and an arm as strong.

At supper Sheela sat on Sir Theodore's right, I on his left, therefore facing her. The meal, as well as I can remember, was simple, but well served and well cooked; and as to attendance, the lame giant seemed to be everywhere at once, and yet nowhere, for he did his duty to perfection, and seemed to obliterate his own presence in doing it.

While I had my cousins to themselves I thought them all that I could desire, but my feelings towards them had undergone a distinct change from the moment of Sheela's reappearance. When I saw that sweet, pure face in the dark doorway, and her swift glance of warning, I felt no doubt whatsoever as to my duty. The right path lay before me, clear, definite, indubitable as the white, straight way over a brown moor. That path I would tread to the end, nothing doubting, and with a proud joy.

And while I so thought, and while such feelings possessed me and filled my mind with a

strong purpose and resolve, came that message
of sheer trust and confidence when, on the
stairs, she sought for my hand in order that, if
but for a few moments, she might feel in con-
tact with truth and loyalty and simple honest
manhood, in this dark den. Now though she
sat before me, not once did her eyes meet
mine. Serene, sweet, and grave, her countenance otherwise betrayed no expression, and
still she spoke only when addressed, and then
no more than courtesy demanded.

Now while Sir Theodore chatted and dis-
pensed the honours of the table with a certain
airy grace, I seemed to test the metal of which
my cousins were composed by the touchstone
supplied by this pure face. That was an unfair
test indeed. How false and hollow I myself
might ring brought to such a test as that, and
yet a consideration so obvious did not occur
to me. The intoxication of love surely had
disordered my faculties ; for what was greater
folly than to judge four men of the world, men
of courts, and camps, and cities, by such a test,
viz., how they looked, and how their influence
affected me when contrasted and compared
with that of a beautiful girl upon whom the

World and Time had never laid its soiling
touch — if Time and the World could stain
such a one—who had been reared, as I might
have guessed, under the purest conditions, and
whom, as my heart told me, I. loved with a
love that would never fail.

In Sir Theodore's lean and dry countenance,
through all its smiling amiability, I seemed
now to catch sight at moments of another
face, in which craft and cruelty predominated.
More than once I thought I saw a look there,
or in his voice heard a tone which, like that
word of sharp authority addressed upstairs to
his youngest son, indicated that this old man,
in spite of his endless anecdotage and tedious
garrulity, was in fact anything but senile.   That
inconsistency I certainly would never have
observed but for the presence of Sheela.

Sir Theodore addressed nearly all his conversation to myself.   Though this was natural,
and indeed no more than courtesy demanded,
yet suddenly the thought flashed upon my
mind, is he studying me ?   Is all this airy
prattle, this gay amiability, this perpetual
pledging, a mere mask under which the real
Sir Theodore is at his ease scrutinising and

taking the measure of his guest and cousin.   I
darted a quick glance at Sheela, no doubt one
of inquiry, as at a trusted friend under enig-
matical circumstances.   A perceptible shadow
of distress or disappointment shivered for a
single instant across her quiet face, leaving it,
however, serene and gentle as before, but
otherwise expressionless.

" Have you ever met heretofore ? " cried Sir
Theodore, with a quick, rasping voice.   The
question leaped from his lips like a sword from
its sheath.

" Alas ! cousin," I replied gaily, and with assumed gallantry, " Time has reserved for me
her chief pleasure till this night.   But why do
you ask ? "

"Oh, nothing, nothing.—And so the Countess
bade her tattling waiting-woman begone—nay,
emphasized the command with a shrewd box
on the ear.   Sir Ulick," said I, " when the news
reached me," &c. &c.

I think my answer, which was literally true,
reassured him.

I was now as wideawake and alert as my
faculties, never very brilliant, would permit.
This prattling, insignificant - looking, elderly

F

cousin of mine was, I felt convinced, an exceedingly clever old man, with infinitely more intellect, penetration, will-power, and force of character than I had given him credit for.   In that swift glance of mine he certainly saw, or thought he saw, something calculated to excite suspicion.   " Seem to observe nothing ; observe all things," were the last words of my child-counsellor.   I had been off my guard when I directed to Sheela that look, the secret of which my cousin had almost penetrated. I would be more careful in future.   I, too, would play a part and match my dull wits, to the best of my ability, against Sir Theodore's. As he was playing the part of a foolish old man, I would play the part of a foolish young one.   He must not be permitted to suspect that he had to do with a vigilant, observant man, whose suspicions had been awakened.

Hitherto I had spoken very little ; now by degrees I began to talk more, and with a certain assumed boyish *abandon* and frankness.

CHAPTER IX

THE CHALLENGE

"I FEAR, cousin," said Sir Theodore, "that you will find time drag heavily here, especially in the evening. Unsuccessful soldiers on the eve of exile are not the pleasantest of company. Do you ever throw a main?"

"Surely," I said; "we played a good deal in the camp before Limerick; I have a few guineas with me, and shall as gladly part with them over the dice-box as in any other way."

"I fear, cousin," replied Sir Theodore, "that we cannot ourselves take up your challenge: neither myself nor my boys would care to play for anything but nominal stakes with one who is at the same time our kinsman and our guest. But stay! now I think of it, I believe Ancient Byrne, who is one of my subalterns, and is quartered in the village at the strand's head, would be glad to oblige you, while we look on and see that all things

are done decently and in order. What say
you, lads ? "

Enoch and Israel expressed a ready assent,
but Immanuel stared at his father with a
puzzled expression of countenance, which I
was at the moment unable to interpret. Supper
being now over, Sir Theodore bade Enoch
cross the sands to the village and tell Ancient
Byrne that a Williamite gentleman now at
Dun-Randal challenged him to a friendly
encounter over the dice-box. "That," he
said, "will bring him down skipping."

He followed Enoch to the castle-door and
a portion of the way over the sands. When
he returned, Immanuel, who still wore that
puzzled expression, said, "But, sir, Ancient
Byrne hath never a shilling. He hath told
me so."

"Not for thee, lad, not for thee," cried Sir
Theodore. "But when a main is to be
thrown, I'll warrant old Felim-na-Cogga" (it
means Felim of the Dice) "will find a forgotten store somewhere."

This was said with a certain resounding
sharpness, and a look which plainly indicated
"Mannie, thou art a fool."

"I confess to you, coz," he added confidentially, turning to me, "that a little affair of this nature greatly exhilarates me—when two good blades cross in earnest, and there is no quarter. I hope you will clear him out, coz; he is a mean wretch for all his good soldiership, and, as Mannie there knows, or will know to-night, one who can bear to see a comrade lack while his own belt is well stuffed."

He ran on in this manner for perhaps a quarter of an hour, his ceaseless random talk almost provoking the suspicion that he had drunk a cup too much. That surmise, however, would not have been just, for he was ever temperate at table, drank little wine, and that well mingled with water. Not only Sheela and myself, but Immanuel too, contemplated him with some surprise. His gaiety was such, that he seemed as if he were about to tread a measure.

At last, drawing his great round watch, he said—

"And Lady Sheela, guardian angel of this Dun unangelic, do thou in the meantime entertain my cousin in thy own withdrawing-room. Play him a sprightly air on thy bandolin, or read him one of thy beloved romances till the trumpet sound battle and onfall."

It may be imagined with what joy I heard this unexpected proposition, the more so as I perceived in Sheela's eyes one quick, sudden flash of pleased surprise. With the prettiest gesture of assent and invitation, she rose and withdrew.

I followed. At the foot of the dark stone flight, Sir Theodore gave me a little pinch as I passed, and winked knowingly.

"Thou hast an eye for a pretty lass, too, coz," he said.

That word went through me like a dagger. Yes, he was a coarse old man for all his dandyism and fashionable airs and graces. For the first time I almost hated him. Possibly my look said so. He turned from me humming—

> "Green sleeves and pudding pies,
> Tell me where my true love lies."

He was indeed in high spirits; evidently an old gamester, in whom the ancient fires had just been rekindled at the prospect of the coming fray.

Far above me I heard the musical patter of Sheela's light experienced feet as she ran up the tortuous stone flight. Once or twice she stopped, as if to make sure that I followed. Followed? Would I not follow her to the world's end? But in the meantime my progress was slow, and I stumbled several times until I learned the trick of the stairs and planted my feet on the outer portions of the steps, for at the inner end they narrowed like the blades of a lady's fan.

At last I came up with her. She was standing at the head of what seemed to be the last flight, and holding a candle in her hand was looking down into the darkness out of which I was emerging. Her face wore a bright and happy expression, altogether different from that which she had exhibited while in the company of the Barretts.

She stamped with her foot. "Make haste, then," she cried; "a snail would have come faster."

She led me into a small room, elegantly furnished, as it seemed to me, and prettily

illuminated with the vari-coloured lights of
shaded candles. A cheerful fire burned upon
a hearth, embracing which ran a chimney-
piece of uncarved black marble. She would
not permit me to close the door. Having
motioned me to a seat with an air of impera-
tiveness, she stood near the entrance while
we conversed, ever and anon listening at the
stairhead. Far below I could hear an obscure
murmur of voices, but nothing more.

This, then, was my lady's bower, where she
dwelt alone with her virgin thoughts and occu-
pations. One still more sacred was suggested
by a hanging curtain crossing the chamber
from wall to wall. On one side were shelves
stored with books in handsome bindings ; near
the chimney-piece a lute or bandolin hung
from a pin in the wall. In a corner stood
a carved and silver-mounted spinning-wheel.
A heap of snow-white carded flax lay beside
it. On the table were painting materials, and
an incomplete painting set on a little table-
easel. It seemed to represent darkness, and
in the midst of the darkness the red glow
of a fire, and figures in chiaroscuro.

"Ah !" she said, coming towards me, "my

grand hiding-place, and last and sure retreat—
the King's Parlour. Would we were there now."

At this moment, to my amazement and dismay, and before I had time to put in words
any of the many questions which thronged
up confusedly in my mind, Sir Theodore cried
up from below—

"Cousin Hugh, cousin Hugh, your man is
on the ground."

"Anon, Sir Theodore ; I am coming."

"One word, Lady Sheela. You fear these
men. What do you fear ?"

She flushed and trembled with passion, and
her eyes flashed.

"They wish to—to—to—me—with that devil.
But I will stab him first."

"Which devil ?"

"Enoch."

In that broken sentence I was able to supply
the word which her virginal pride would not
permit her to utter.

Now I heard impatient steps on the stair.
It was Sir Theodore hastening to fetch me
down. As I turned to leave she sprang
forward, took one of my hands in both of
hers, and said in a low voice—

"We are comrades and friends, are we not?"

"As God lives," I said. I was under the glamour of her sex and youth and beauty, and at the moment saw all things with her eyes.

"And for your life's sake," she whispered, "don't seem to suspect. Maintain in all things your seeming—friendly attitude to—these—devils."

I was met on the stairs by Sir Theodore, who conducted me to that withdrawing-room already described, where he gaily introduced me to my antagonist. To the eye this personage looked no way formidable—seemingly an old ale-house Ancient, slovenly, sullen, coarse, and even vulgar in appearance, though Sir Theodore kept assuring me that he was of a most ancient and honourable house.

"As good as the Barretts, any way," quoth the Ancient sulkily.

"Better, man, better," cried Sir Theodore gaily, "being old Milesian, not modern Norman. But stir thyself and get to work. Gods! how briskly, in my own hot youth, I would come to a meeting of this nature."

My opponent's right hand was all swathed into shapelessness. " Bitch of a pistol," he explained laconically, and with a dull and sulky look at Sir Theodore, which I could not interpret, though it seemed to have meaning in it. Disabled in this manner, it was but natural that he should get some one to throw for him. Enoch threw.

CHAPTER X

THE BATTLE, AND AFTER

WE, the gladiators of the evening, having first pledged each other and made polite speeches, slung our belts upon the table, my opponent's seemingly as well filled as my own. This latter preliminary was, when I was young, expected to be discharged in a high, fierce, belligerent manner, though I hear that a less braggadocio style has since come into vogue. But a dicing encounter was a very serious affair indeed when the right royal faces of William and Mary adorned the obverse side of our guineas. The Ancient, though he did pledge me, mumbled his courtesy-speech in an indistinct manner, and showed no alacrity or spirit in tabling his gold. I thought he was afraid, and had no great spirit for the encounter. As usual I was wrong, and even absurdly wrong. At twenty-one a youth is by a legal fiction supposed to be a man. I am very certain that at twenty-three I was a mere boy, and a very dull boy, too. One of my childish foibles was family pride. I can still remember the air and manner with which I used to speak of my "West country Jacobite kinsmen," as if the fact that any one who belonged to my house were of itself a sufficient guarantee of honour and reputation. One of my duels, which numbered three so far, was fought with a Swedish officer called Ericson, who had reflected on the honour (as Jacobites) of these same kinsmen. Enough.

The Ancient commenced work by a deep draught at his tankard, and afterwards drank steadily all the night ; indeed, he appeared to me to take more interest in his claret than in his play.

" A very seasoned old gamester—a cool hand, if there be one," explained Sir Theodore to me from time to time, when I contemplated, with more than usual surprise, that apathetic and far from alluring countenance, in which the nose beamed instead of the eyes, which ignoble organ indeed, I mean the nose, grew brighter and brighter as the night advanced.

The play proceeded with varying fortune.

Once nearly half my opponent's store seemed to be at my side of the table, and true to my boyish rôle, I rejoiced and vaunted greatly, but by degrees my luck left me, and, as it drew towards midnight, I became painfully aware that I had but three guineas left. After that I seemed to recover ; and when Sir Theodore, striking his bony fist on the table, declared that the war was over for the present, I found that I had still remaining twenty-five guineas, having lost exactly one hundred and eighty, for I began with two hundred and five.

"Well, coz," said Sir Theodore, "Fortune, the jade, has played thee a nasty trick this night ; but thou shalt beat him yet, I promise you. What ! don't be cast down, lad. A check is not a defeat."

Ancient Byrne did not appear to be much elated either by his victory or by the enormous quantity of claret which he had silently consumed during the evening. He was plainly a very seasoned hand, both at dicing and drinking.

Sir Theodore had been watching the play attentively throughout. Enoch had rattled and shed forth the dice on behalf of the

Ancient, and did so with all the appearance of a veteran practitioner. Once when things were going dead against me, he used some phrases of condolence, to which, from the ingle-nook, where Immanuel sat nodding and almost quite drunk, came like an echo, in a thick, tipsy voice, the words—

"And Enoch walked with God."

Enoch said nothing, but his countenance showed that he was not one who relished being the subject of a "quiz." The Ancient, however, in spite of his claret, saw and enjoyed this questionable joke, and laughed gleefully.

The lame man had laid some cold collation for us at a sideboard, and there, amid such conversation as may be imagined, this to me disastrous evening came to an end. But, indeed, I was not over-much concerned, for the guineas which I lost had, in fact, been intended by me for a gift. Moreover, my mind all through had been as much preoccupied with the Lady Sheela de Stanton as my opponent's apparently had been with the fascinations of my kinsman's claret.

In the end he rose, exhibiting a thick-set

and strong, if somewhat shapeless, figure, and
in a husky voice said—

"Immanuel, your arm."

"But Immanuel is as unsteady on his legs
as yourself, Ancient," remarked Israel. "Better
take mine."

"Young man," replied the Ancient, looking
full at Israel, while he endeavoured to balance
himself on widely dispread feet—"young man,
d—d—drunk or s—sober, I prefer Immanuel."

Then he turned to me, and raising his
plumed hat, which he had worn all the evening, addressed me, tipsily indeed, yet not without a certain dignity—

"Lieutenant Netterville, you are a d—d—
damned Williamite, no doubt ; I suppose, you
cannot help that ; you were b—born so.   But
you are a man of honour and a gentleman, as
I am myself, as I am myself ; within l—limits.
And whenever it is your good p—p—pleasure
to vary the entertainment and change ivory
for s—steel, why then, sir, Felim-na-Cogga
is at your service, and the sands here are
h—h—hard and l—l—level."

Casting a very watery and yet defiant eye
on Sir Theodore, and leaning on the not very

assistful arm of Immanuel, this curious specimen of Jacobite chivalry slowly and labo-
riously withdrew.   My cousins invited me to
enjoy the spectacle of the pair crossing the
sands under the light of the moon, but I
would not.

Sir Theodore's countenance, when he referred
to the events of the evening, wore indeed an
expression of sympathy, but he was, in fact, as
jocund as a shepherd at a fair.   Evidently a
seasoned old gamester, and one who dearly
loved a dicing duel.

"Thou wilt clear him out the morrow in
fine style," he said.   "Thou wilt break the
battle on him," &c. &c.

"I wish Ancient Byrne joy of my guineas,"
I said.   "For myself, I care not if I ever meet
him again."

"Nay, nay, man," cried Sir Theodore reso-
nantly.   "We shall talk the matter over anon.
Now for bed."

G

CHAPTER XI

THE HONOUR OF THE BARRETTS

WHEN I returned to the solitude of my chamber, which I did with joy, it was not to reflect upon my losses and the decisive victory gained over me by that absurd antagonist, but to think about Sheela, to live over again the events of the night and evening so far as she was concerned, and to conjure up in imagination her every word, look, and gesture. Love truly had taken me at last, not a struggling captive, in his golden toils.

What bright intelligence shone from those eyes! What spirit and purpose, what tenderness of affection dwelt in that gentle heart, for I had not forgotten how the tears filled her eyes when she mentioned the name of her lost brother. Cultivated, too, and refined I perceived her to be. Her lute, her painting materials, that curious picture, her books—romance literature, as Sir Theodore's suggestion implied—the elegance and taste shown in the decoration and arrangement of her little withdrawing-room, her spinning-wheel and carded flax, showed one who, in this savage region, cultivated those humane studies and graceful or serviceable feminine accomplishments which add such a charm to womanhood. Lady Sheela de Stanton had not wanted all due education and instruction. And she would stab "that devil." Yes; Enoch as a bridegroom would not fare well. There were other elements in the being of this beautiful creature which I less understood, but reflected upon with a certain awe. Her days and nights on the salt water. What did that mean? this love for the barren, bitter, restless sea, so melancholy, wild, savage, and cruel. I had had but one experience of the sea so far, and did not like it. It was during that disastrous campaign in which Schomberg was our general. I was ordered to sail with my company from Carrickfergus to Dublin. We went very near to being drowned on that occasion, and this, my sole experience of the salt water, gave me quite a horror of the element. Yet Sheela spent her days and nights in mysterious

communion with that savage power, whose
brightness and glitter seemed to me like the
glossy sheen of the tiger's fur. And in Sheela,
too, I was aware of something mysterious and
remote, as if that dread element had communicated to her a share of its own untamable
power. Yet, on the other hand, what simpli-
city and naturalness were hers! I recalled
the tears, brighter than dew-drops, which
started from her eyes when she spoke of her
"dear brother." I recalled that beautiful
trustfulness with which, childlike, she had
felt for my hand in the darkness, to reassure
herself of my presence and proximity.

But when I recalled this singular incident
my heart seemed to chill. That action proved
that the bare thought of me as a man, and
of herself as a woman, never once crossed
her mind. No doubt she did regard me as
a child might her nurse or mother, her
father or her very elder brother. She was
no more than fifteen, and I was twenty-
three. What a chasm and gulf of time must
all those years seem to her. I was dull of
wit, hugely big and corporeal, and as to my
face—indeed, I had not the least notion

whether I was good-looking or the reverse, probably the latter. A florid visage adorned with innocent blue eyes was all my glass ever showed me.

Matchless, incomparable in beauty, goodness, and nobility of soul, she seemed to me. Again I thought of her, and continued to think of her, as the star which I had seen shining over the black battlements. The black battlements! Here I thought of Sir Theodore and his three handsome sons, all so kind and cordial to me, their unknown Williamite cousin.

Had they not this very night shown a nice sense of honour in peremptorily declining a kinsman's challenge to play, and in introducing a stranger to win my money or lose his own?

How, in a heart so pure and good as hers, could such an irrational dislike and suspicion of my kinsmen have taken root? All this I attributed to her foster-brother. It was he who sowed those ill seeds in that pure soil, meant by the Almighty to grow only rare flowers of love and courtesy and all sweet and amiable things. I waxed wroth with this

foster-brother and with the custom, too pre-
valent in Ireland, of admitting such persons to
intimacy and confidence.   And yet, might not
the Barretts, by putting forward Enoch as an
aspirant for her hand, quite naturally pro-
voke a just wrath and abhorrence in that
pure soul and proud spirit, and so, without
deserving it, become to her objects of pro-
found suspicion in everything ? All manner
of dim thoughts and emotions played ceaselessly through my mind.   Nevertheless, on the
whole, my spirit overflowed with joy, and a
thousand times I felicitated myself on my
acceptance of Sir Theodore's kind invitation,
so that even the booming of the Atlantic, the
long roar of the tide upon the strand, and
the wild cries of those uncanny birds out
there in the night and the darkness, seemed a
soothing music.   The purple light of love was
in me and around me as I sank to sleep
that night.

I was awakened by a gay voice at my bed-
side ; it was Sir Theodore's.   Though still
early, indeed only glimmering dawn, he was
not only up, but dressed to perfection, and
looking fresh and rosy.   He sat familiarly at

the foot of my bed, and spoke in a cheery and encouraging manner about the events of last night. He did not know how little I regarded them.

"Hugh, dear lad," he said, "it will not do at all to let that rascal Ancient get the better of us so. Lay you in another last of munition, return to the charge, and storm him right out of his works."

"But, Sir Theodore," I replied, laughing, "I have no more at hand. My treasure is at Athlone, and, indeed, I feel no ambition to win a victory over your bibulous Ancient."

"No, no, no, cousin. The honour of the house is concerned. We are all eager, believe me, to see this affront to Dun-Randal wiped out without delay. My son Israel, getting a written order from you upon your goldsmith, will ride to Athlone, and be back by six of the clock. My sons and I will be abroad to-day. You will pardon us the seeming inattention, but ere we sail we have divers matters to settle with certain of the gentry of the province. My fair ward and you shall be our garrison. Yes, yes, you must overthrow the

Ancient this night.   See, I have the writing materials at hand, and Izzie "—(so he called Israel)—" is booted and spurred, and his horse at the door ready to start."

Obviously Sir Theodore was very much bent on this business.   Influenced by some vague apprehension that my refusal might lead to a change in his plans, I yielded, and, half-dressed as I was by this time, I went to the table where the writing materials were already invitingly dispread, and wrote an order to Master Simon Petty at the sign of the Lamb, in the way of the Saxons (*Srad-na-Sassenagh* it was more generally called), directing him to hand to bearer for my use two hundred and fifty guineas, and to regard his quittance as my own.

Sir Theodore strode humming around the room, but paused when my pen wandered to the left-hand lower corner of the sheet.

" A private mark, I presume," he said.

" Yes," I replied.   " Master Petty is bound by our terms to honour absolutely, and at once, any draft bearing this mark."

. He sanded the script himself, letting his eyes wander over the contents.

"Nay, lad," he said, "write in five hundred guineas in lieu of the smaller sum, subscribing thy name to the erasure. It is incredible what runs of luck, adverse and toward, will happen in such encounters, and this rascal, I know him, will not play less than the gold be tabled, and glittering before his eyes—a very scurvy, suspicious fellow."

"Nay, cousin," I said, "I shall not alter it."

He seized my arm while he again declaimed on the advisability of laying in a good store of munition. Slight as he was, and, to the eye, giving no great promise of strength, the old man's grip was like iron. This, and something domineering in the sound of his voice, aroused certain little sleeping devils within me, and I answered very quietly, but in a tone which there was no mistaking—

"No, Sir Theodore, I shall not alter what I have written."

The sound of my voice startled him. I think he did not look to find in me any resolution. "Ha," he said, and his eyes became like two little glittering points.

Then more cheerily, and in his natural tones, "Very well, coz, as you like."

Indeed, I was but a poor actor. Last night I had talked like a boy, now I had behaved with the independence and resolution of a man.

CHAPTER XII

DRAWING TO THE CRISIS

SHEELA appeared at the breakfast-table very grave and quiet, as was her manner before my kinsmen. She would scarcely speak to me. That I did not so much mind, for I looked forward now with glad anticipation to a whole day spent in her company. But I was to experience a bitter disappointment. Sir Theodore, accompanied by Enoch and Immanuel, and attended by a troop of half-a-dozen horsemen, set out from the castle shortly after breakfast. Before starting he took me aside.

"There is a promise," he said, "which my relations with this young lady compel me to exact from you, my dear cousin, although it may not be altogether welcome or agreeable to yourself. In short, I have to request you to give me your word of honour that you will not, save in my presence, hold any com-

munication with my young ward, the Lady
Sheela de Stanton." He filled towards her
now, he said, the place of Baron Raymond
her brother. She was little more than a
child, very beautiful, heiress-prospective to
enormous estates, &c. &c.

Nothing remained for me save to give that
promise. Sir Theodore was evidently a very
strict guardian, and indeed, though I might
lament his preciseness, I could not censure
it. From the battlements of the castle, where
I spent much of that morning, I could see
Sheela cross the sands ; two armed men went
before and two followed. Afterwards I saw
her row out in her little curragh from a
beach which lay towards the west, and was
separated from our sandy shore by a spit of
rocky land. It lay due south from that square
house already referred to. I could see her
lithe, graceful figure as it swayed, and the
flashing of her little white paddles. A well-
manned boat also put out there, and followed,
though at a respectful distance. Sir Theodore
certainly seemed to take very good care of
his ward. Then a dark promontory concealed
curragh and boat, while I stared ruefully at

the glittering sea. It may be imagined how
I felt.

Just then, and for the first time, it occurred
to me that the behaviour of my cousins was,
to say the least, singular. Without making
any provision whatever for my diversion and
amusement, and having debarred me utterly
from all intercourse with the one person in
Dun-Randal whose society would naturally
be pleasing to a young man, they had coolly
departed for the day. Israel indeed had
apparently gone on my business, but really
on Sir Theodore's, who plainly derived an
incredible degree of pleasure from a dicing-
war fought *à outrance*. Duelling and single
combats of all kinds are no doubt dear to
the unregenerate heart of man, and yet it
did not seem very kind or considerate on
his part to thrust me into an affair of this
kind, which might end in my ruin, or that of
one of his own officers. Israel, I say, might
possibly be excused, on the ground that he
had left Dun-Randal in order to serve me.
But Sir Theodore himself, with Enoch and
Immanuel, had certainly gone off on their
own business or pleasure without inviting

me to accompany them. Had the Barretts
been my guests at Lissanare, as I was theirs
at Dun-Randal, would I have treated them
so? Surely not. But for Sheela, I might
have shaken from my feet the sands of Dun-
Randal this day. Love and wrath held alter-
nate possession of my mind, while from time
to time the emptiness and desolation of the
surrounding country struck a chill into my
heart. There, too, on the white sands, exactly
in the same posture, sat the lonely watcher,
waiting for "her man" and "the day of Judgment," young, beautiful, and insane, Israel's
work. No cheerful feature indeed in the rueful
landscape was that poor creature.

At last descending from the battlements,
I took from my saddle-bags a little pocket
Virgil, and sitting by the withdrawing-room
fire, sought to compose my mind by reading,
but could hardly see the print, so many faces
came between me and it.

Then I said that I would walk off the excitement, go in a westerly direction along
the cliffs, and if I could not speak with Sir
Theodore's ward, who held all my heart in her
two white hands, at least see her, though as

a speck in the grey ocean. To the hunger of love the smallest crumb is welcome, and, when compared with nothing, almost a banquet.

As I passed through the great hall I noticed that our ward was increased. There were two soldiers there, fully armed. They rose and saluted me respectfully as I passed.

Crossing the sands, I paused before the square house. To me now it was an object of the deepest interest since I learned that it was Sheela's home. Blessings on every stone of it! I perceived there many indications of elegance and refinement, defaced, however, by recent neglect. I looked like a lover on all these visible emanations of a beautiful soul. My darling had not only dwelt here, but had in a measure caused this one corner of the savage region to become the mirror of her own sweet spirit. The house was uninhabited, and the windows shuttered. Here, too, the aspect of things was melancholy; here, too, the curse which brooded over the whole country had fallen.

It occurred to me as strange that the Barretts should not have taken up their abode in this inhabited and commodious house, instead of in that dreary keep. But there was so much that was puzzling in the behaviour of my cousins, that one unexplained circumstance the more made little difference. Delaying here for a while I continued my walk ; but ere leaving the little demesne with its low, dry-stone wall, over which I leaped, I caught sight of a well-mounted dragoon on the edge of the little scrubby wood, half concealed amongst the trees, fully armed. Looking backwards I saw the two soldiers who had saluted me in the castle-hall standing now before the door, their faces in my direction. Was I watched ? From Sheela's house a little road ran down to a pebbly strand, on which drawn up I saw many boats. It was from this strand she had rowed out. Climbing a steep eminence which rose here I could see far away westward her curragh and herself like a speck, and, hard by, the guarding boat.

Long before the short day grew to dusk she returned. True to my word, I made no attempt to meet her or speak with her. When I myself came back, which was at nightfall, the soldiers were not in the great hall, but as I went upstairs I heard them below me talking with the lame giant Fergananim. Fergananim, I may explain, means "The man without a name," *i.e.*, Fer-gan-anim. It was not an uncommon name in Ireland when I was young.

I found Israel in the withdrawing-room. As he gave me my gold, he said with a knowing air, "Thy banker, cousin Hugh, hath a fair daughter, a marvellous comely wench."

"Yes," I said coldly, pouching my guineas, "Mistress Kate Petty is what you say, and her father, though a merchant, wears a sword, and can use it."

Israel's meaning looks, and his dull black eyes, kindling with a new lustful flame, were at the moment inexpressibly odious to me. Had he added another word, I believe I would have told him so. I left him on the spot, preferring the cold of my chamber to his society, and did not return to the withdrawing-room till the reappearance of Sir Theodore and the two other sons.

They were all in high spirits, owing, I think, to the events of the day; but would talk of nothing but of the approaching fray, in which

H

I was to do mighty things, clear out the Ancient utterly, and restore the credit of Dun-Randal.

I must now pretermit many particulars while I hasten on to the catastrophe. In spite of my cousins' cheerful and unanimous prognostications, this evening my dicing war with the bibulous Ancient repeated almost exactly the event of its predecessor. But I did not mind it; I had seen a face, and listened to accents, compared with which gold was dross. I had had some conversation with Sheela, though in the presence of her guardian.

Now, although I was this night again disastrously beaten, and although my cousins used many expressions of condolence, I could perceive that they were all, in fact, in high spirits. Evidently their visit to the neighbouring gentry had resulted so much to their satisfaction, that they had little room left in their minds to feel any concern about myself. Then as day followed day they seemed gradually to discard from their manners much of that dignity, repose, and self-restraint, nay, in a quite noticeable degree, much even of the politeness which they had exhibited on

the night of my arrival, and their merriment
jarred upon me. Sir Theodore, too, redoubled
his airs of paternal and old-fashioned gallantry
towards his young ward. Once or twice his
manner towards her filled me with a sudden
sense of horror. I dared not confess to my
mind in words what it seemed to suggest.
The young men laughed a good deal among
themselves, seeming to enjoy together something of an amusing nature, in the knowledge
of which I was not allowed to share, gross
ill-breeding as I felt it to be. Once, after
Sheela's withdrawal from the supper-table,
Israel talked so freely about women, that I
wondered his father did not rebuke and restrain him.

He, however, only said airily, turning to
myself—

"I often tell him that some morning he will
be found with a knife between his ribs."

"I should not be surprised," I said coldly.

For a few days nothing occurred to break
the monotony. The Barretts left home every
morning. I spent my days solitary, and in
the evenings lost heavily to the Ancient,
paying him in drafts upon my goldsmith,

which were duly honoured, no doubt, for I heard of no difficulty. My genius of ill-fortune seemed to have secured an effectual lodgment in those little ivory cubes. Never once, even for a single instant, did I suspect foul play, neither did I now so much resent the behaviour of my cousins in absenting themselves with such regularity in order to attend to their own business. For that Sir Theodore had apologised, explaining that their business with those neighbouring magnates was of the most vital importance. But I did keenly resent what I conceived to be an undoubted falling away of that personal courtesy which was at first shown me in Dun-Randal. As will be remembered, even on the morning after my arrival I observed something harsh, sharp, and peremptory in the tones of Sir Theodore ; and now one night, I think it was the fourth, while urging me to double the stakes for which Ancient Byrne and myself had hitherto played, both his manner and his matter were anything but those of one gentleman addressing another. When I looked at him, possibly with a kindling eye, he apologised, but I could not forget such an incident. The young men too, as I have said, showed in many small ways a lack of their former courtesy and graciousness. Under such circumstances, I was now of course a trespasser on their hospitality. If, as their manner seemed to indicate, they wished me to leave, it was my duty to leave.

Love, and love alone, chained me here. To see and speak with Sheela, even under such starving conditions as Sir Theodore had imposed, was to me an abundant reward for my heavy pecuniary losses. But even for love's sweet sake I could not endure such a loss of honour as was involved in a visit prolonged after the welcome of my hosts seemed to be exhausted, and when courtesy was actually changing to something very like discourtesy.

One day Sir Theodore received visitors. The leader of this party, which from the battlements I saw ride across the sands, was a great burly and bearded person, rough of manner, loud of voice, Lord ——, one of the great guns of the west. I knew him well by name and appearance, and also was aware that, owing to past services, he possessed much influence with the authorities. As he entered

Dun-Randal his voice seemed to rumble in every nook and cranny of the castle. Swearing as he came, he passed my room and remained for a few minutes in Sheela's withdrawing-room, where he talked much and loudly, and, as I thought, in a bullying fashion.

Returning, he met Sir Theodore on my landing, where I heard him say—

"Set fair in this quarter, Sir Theodore."

Together they then entered Sir Theodore's bedchamber, whence I seemed to hear the noise of the counting of money. As they came out I heard our great guest say in his thunder tones—

"You are a damned Jacobite, Sir Theodore, but by God you are a gentleman, and you shall be one of us. That I swear."

Again as they descended I heard him say—

"But a looser rein, Sir Theodore, a looser rein ; less surveillance, espionage, and all that. The darlings will have their little notions and fancies."

What did it all mean ?

There followed something which I did not hear—a coarse jest, I suppose, for the laughter which succeeded almost shook the castle, the roar of our mighty man mingling with the thinner cachinnations of my cousin.

A mid-day collation, to which I was not invited, nor in which, if invited, I would have participated, came next, with noise enough to wake the Seven Sleepers. When our guests departed there was a great silence in the castle, amid which I heard two low sounds—that of my cousins conversing below, and of Sheela sobbing above.

One thing amazed and confounded me. After this Sheela hardly answered when I spoke to her, while her manner underwent a singular alteration towards Sir Theodore. She seemed to accept with equanimity, almost to welcome, those attentions and gallantries which to me seemed so unspeakably revolting.

Next day, as I took my now daily solitary walk, it seemed to me that the surrounding country exhibited signs of improvement. I saw cattle in some of the fields. Many deserted houses, by their smoke and otherwise, showed symptoms of reoccupation. Also I heard one of two peasants who passed me observe to the other in Gaelic, "Well, he's not so bad after all, be the reason of the change what it may."

Also I saw carpenters and masons at work about Baronscourt, and a laden dray at the door.

That same evening, it was the fifth, Sheela came to the supper-table with a book in her hand, and asked Sir Theodore to translate a Latin phrase which occurred in her reading.

"I can translate what I see in beautiful live eyes," he replied, with an odious air and look of gallantry, "but spare me the dead languages."

Then she seemed to lose her place, but found it again, and reached the book to me.

"Yes," I said, "a common quotation, 'Whom the gods wish to destroy they first make mad.'" I was about to return her the book when I observed in pencil marks on the margin "*Tu captivus es.*" I only bowed and returned the volume.

That night I again lost heavily. "This dicing affair grows tedious," exclaimed Sir Theodore testily, after the departure of the Ancient. "Double the stakes to-morrow night and bring the matter to an end."

"That proposal I decline," I said coldly.

"My officers speak of you as hare-hearted," he replied.

"From the only specimen I have met," I retorted, "I care little how your officers speak of me. In any case, I would decline to make myself a pauper for the sake of a word. And I will say something else," I added, for my temper was now thoroughly roused, "I shall play no more. If you wish to avenge the honour of Dun-Randal upon your Ancient, play yourselves."

CHAPTER XIII

GAYEST OF CONQUERORS AND BRIDEGROOMS

A SILENCE fell upon the party when I said this. I spoke strongly, I dare say passionately, for indeed I felt indignant enough. The thought, "Am I, or am I not a prisoner," had not left my mind all the evening. I resolved to test that question at once.

"Sir Theodore," I said, "the air of this room is close, and I am somewhat fretted. I shall walk on the sands for a little time before going to rest."

"Nay, sir. No one leaves my castle to-night. If thou art heated, walk on the battlements. It is cooler there."

There was a sharp edge upon his voice as he said this. I looked at him steadily, then at the two young men Enoch and Israel, for Immanuel had just left the room. On their hard, relentless faces I seemed to detect the flicker of a smile. Every hand, too, including the old man's, was in proximity with the sword-grip. So, for that matter, was my own. I dare say my countenance was not quite seraphic to look upon, but dark and dangerous exceedingly, for I was conscious of a very black and ungovernable tide of wrath mounting up within me from the inner deeps.

"Sir Theodore," I cried, "as you are a man and a gentleman, answer me true. Am I your prisoner?"

So saying, I grasped my sword-hilt to draw, and drew—the hilt.

Mocking faces were the last sight which I saw, and a peal of mocking laughter the last sound which I heard, for from behind some one who at that moment entered struck me. I remember no more.

When I came to myself I was in darkness. The first thing of which I was conscious was the pain in my head. As I raised my hand to the aching part I heard the rattle of iron, and felt an unusual weight at my wrists. I was in handlocks, and chained besides. When I tried to rise, I found that my ankles were gyved also. To the footlocks there was an attached chain. I drew it towards me till it became taut. Exerting my strength, it seemed to yield, and I drew in something heavy which clattered on the stone floor. It was a cannon ball. Yes, I was a prisoner, and a moderately well secured one, too. Groping around in the darkness, I discovered by certain signs that I was in my own bedroom. Finding my bed, I sat down there and endeavoured to collect my thoughts, rueful and haggard as they were, and to realise my very dismal situation. It was a bitter reflection that I had brought all this upon myself by my foolish pride, for of warnings I had received enough to set any one endowed with the least prudence upon his guard. What were my cousins' intentions towards me ? It was a question which I could not resolve without their assistance, and that no doubt would be forthcoming with daylight. To add to all my other misery, I was suffering from an intolerable thirst. No doubt I had bled freely from that wound in my head, for my clothes were quite drenched with blood. There was no water in the room. I learned that in the course of my gropings. At last I lay down, still anchored, so to speak,

to my cannon-ball, and in spite of my thirst
and the irons fell into a troubled sleep, interrupted with dreams of lakes and fountains,
from which I seemed to drink insatiably.

When I awoke I could see the window with
its one bar. It was growing towards morning. I felt now for that little gift, talisman,
or what not, which Sheela had sewn into the
lining of my coat on the first night that I slept
in Dun-Randal, and was rejoiced to find it
safe, the more so, inasmuch as all my pockets
had been rifled. That little talisman indeed I
had never forgotten, and was very well aware
of its exact position, though I had resolved
never to look at it till the situation which she
seemed to predict might arise. It consisted
only of a little coil of strong thread, to which
was attached a leaden weight or sinker. "Sir
Untrustful Proud," such were my darling's
words, "thou mayest find a humble but good
ally in this little gift when thy pride and self-
confidence are brought down to the dust.
Some time you may find yourself fishing with
it for your life."

Surely now I was brought down to the
dust.

How came Sheela to have this little engine of lead and thread on her person when she met me for the first time. Plainly for her own use. I entertained no doubt as to what that use was. The little sinker brought down the thread and held it straight. Watched and warded as she was, she had thus provided herself with means of intercourse with the outer world, and her friends there. So, through Sheela's prophetic mind it had flashed, that possibly I might be confined in this or some other upper chamber. Therefore she had given me the little engine whereby she was in the habit of communicating with outside friends, probably with her foster-brother. What a gleam of all but preternatural foresight was evident in that sudden and prompt action on her part. At a glance she saw that, as I in no way resembled my cousins, I was here, not as an ally and confederate, but as a victim. Quick to decide and act, as quick to perceive, know, and understand, my beautiful one, without the hesitation of a single moment, had put into my possession a possible means of communication with those who were in communication with her. As I was

about to let my leaded line fall I heard Fergananim moving heavily below, and other
sounds which indicated that my cousins too
were stirring.   Then quite near me I heard
Sir Theodore's voice, high, shrieky, unmelo-
dious, yet animated, uplifted in a gay matin
song.   Surely too there is, as I have heard,
a " peace of the devil which passeth all understanding."   Indeed, I feel quite certain that
this utterly unprincipled old man was far
happier than many an upright and honourable gentleman whom I have known.   Perhaps the children of the Devil are wiser in
their generation than the children of light,
and, sometimes at least, contrive to avoid
ground where the more generous and warm-
hearted ones stumble and fall.   For example,
Sir Theodore was a rascal, but temperate.
Enoch was a water-drinker, so was Israel.
At breakfast, the noises of which I could hear,
the whole party seemed very gay and hilarious.
After breakfast I was visited by Sir Theodore,
accompanied by his big henchman, the nameless one.   Sir Theodore bore writing-materials,
which he laid on the table.

"You see, cousin," he began, quite in a

paternal tone, "what you have brought upon yourself by your very foolish conduct. That blow now—you struck too hard, Fergananim, much too hard—went near to being your *coup de grace*, and would in that event have quite spoiled my plans. Had you been a man of sense you would have perceived, from certain very evident signs and tokens, that it was my purpose, in a perfectly quiet and gentleman-like manner, to convey all that Williamite treasure of yours to my own loyal exchequer. With half an eye, a man of less intelligence than you might have seen all that, and yielded gracefully to the necessities of the situation. But you would not, or could not.   Hence results.   You will now sit down at this table and write a letter which I shall dictate, direct-ing Master Petty to send hither all the moneys which you committed to his keeping, it being your intention, so you will write, to sail hence for the Continent, and not from Dublin."

"And what if I refuse ?" I replied quietly, by a powerful effort controlling my wrath.

"Refuse ! refuse ! S'death, man, you can't refuse. If you refuse, by the Son of God, I

will tear you limb from limb on the rack. I
have one in the cellar, well oiled and working freely."

That, then, was the novel warlike engine
over which I had puzzled on the first night.
"I have found it useful," he went on, "in
compelling the rustic misers hereaway to disgorge and deliver up their secret hoards.
Consult your own pleasure then, my dear
cousin. If you are for the rack, say so, and
my Hercules here, assisted if necessary by
my lusty brood, Enoch, Israel, and Immanuel,
will carry you thither like a babe. Remember
always, dear coz, that here you are no more
than a sparrow in a hawk's claws."

"Let me have a few minutes to consider,"
I replied, "and in the meantime some water
to drink."

I was faint and wretched. Truly I have
not often shown a spirit so weak as I did
this day.

"Ha! You thirst! Is that so? You lost
blood last night! Fergananim, my soul, you
struck too hard. Yet see how Divine Pro-
vidence brings forth good results, even out
of blunders and excesses. Thirst, then—thirst

I

will do my work far better than the rack. I
was thirsty once myself. It was in the Castle
of Spandau. And I had an adventure there
too—a woman in it, quite a romantic affair, I
can assure you, though I had to kill her afterwards. It was a pity, for she was a fine
woman, and fond of me, but one or other of
us had to die, and I have always contrived
during my life to take uncommon good care
of myself. Yes, I know what thirst is, and
now we can reduce this controversy to a
matter of bargain and sale. You give me
the script, and I give you water. No script,
no water."

"You look like a man," I said, speaking
very slowly, "yet I think there is not in Hell
a greater devil."

"My dear cousin, you wander from the
point," he replied, smiling; "I am as God made
me. You have really nothing of which you
can justly complain. Your Netterville estates
are rightly mine. They went to your branch
—the spindle branch—of the family because
your grandfather was a rebel, and drew his
traitor sword for the rebel and tyrant, Crom-
well! By a stratagem I recover them in the

form of gold, a much more convenient kind of property in our times—recover them from a young man of weak understanding, though of great bodily size and strength, a man of honour too, and nice feelings, as I frankly admit. But—but—war, cousin, takes many shapes, and stratagem is a quite honourable weapon in these days. Nay, nay, cousin, stir not one step. Desperate men will resort to desperate remedies."

I was moving towards him insensibly, as I thought; but this old man had the eyes of a lynx.

He plucked out a pistol as he spoke.

" Now, cousin, let's to business. Know, then, that even without thy assistance this treasure is mine. My son Enoch, the sweetest of boys, very adroit and intelligent, and without vice, hath a very pretty hand, and can counterfeit a signature so as to deceive the rightful owner; and I know thy private mark. Sign, then, and suffer not, for not signing will not avail."

" I am powerless in your hands," I replied, "and tortured with thirst. Give me water, and I shall sign what you will." I was not indeed conquered, but I wished to gain time. My clue would be useless in the cellars, to which he had threatened to transfer me.

When I had duly written and signed and sealed the letter, and been relieved of my anguish arising from thirst, I conversed with him calmly, endeavouring even to imitate his own jocular style.

"Tell me now," I said frankly, "Sir Theodore, what are your intentions towards me."

"There is nothing so good as clear, upright, and straightforward dealing," he said, "between man and man, and particularly between kinsmen. My present purpose is to blow up the castle on the eve of my sons' departure. You will be in the dungeon when that event takes place, after which you will sleep peacefully through the centuries with a few thousand tons of masonry above you. You see now to what extremities you have reduced me by your folly. I don't want your life ; it is of no service to me. But dead men tell no tales. I shall be happier in Baronscourt with my sweet bride, and my dear boys happier abroad, you being dumb till Judgment Day. But don't be cast down, coz.

Death comes to all—sooner or later to all. You are a soldier, and will doubtless find it less disagreeable than others do.   Death ! a fico for it.   Puff, and all's over."

His garrulity was such that I hoped to make my account of it by encouraging him to talk.   He was just now very talkative and vainglorious.

"My disappearance will be inquired into," I said.   "My King's arm is long enough to pluck at least murderers out of the Spanish king's hands."

"I am not a simpleton, coz.   I have provided for all that.   We have your letter to Master Simon Petty to show that you sailed into Spain with my sons.   Enoch will contrive all that remains."

"You are certainly frank, Sir Theodore. May I ask what are your intentions towards the young lady ?"

"To marry her, lad, nothing more.   Not for the world would I hurt a hair of her beautiful head."

I sprang to my feet with a cry. Sir Theodore darted back a pace or two. At the sound of my voice and the clanking of

my chains the grim henchman reappeared.
"Steady there or I fire," cried Sir Theodore.
He had me covered as he spoke. "That
will do, Fergananim dear. You may retire.
Yes, Hugh Netterville," he went on, glory-
ing in his wickedness, "since your oppor-
tune arrival I have altered all my plans very
much for the better. Once Enoch was to
have married the young lady, while I sailed
away with the rents and treasure. Now I
remain at home, a happy bridegroom, with
your treasure, coz. I have secured friends
who will make my peace with the Government.
And as to the young lady's friends, those of
them that are of any worth I have secured
them in like manner; also by her brother's
written directions that she shall marry me,
and so heal feuds between our houses as old
as the days of King Hal. Enoch, as I have
already told you, hath a very pretty hand.
The Baron dies abroad without heirs. *Voilà
tout!* So saith rumour. Fact, on the contrary,
avers, though none will heed, that he died at
home. Of course you will see now that the
Ancient was a mere instrument in my hands,
poor, honest, crapulous devil, as mechanical

and unresisting as a quill in the hands of that
sweet boy Enoch ; though he did scratch and
splutter a little in the use.   'Bitch of a pistol.'
Ha, ha !   It is an amazement to me, cousin,
how a man can sink to such a depth of sim-
plicity as yours."

"One form of misery at least you can spare
me," I cried in anguish.

"What is that ?"

"Your presence."

"'Fore God, not a reasonable request, seeing
that my pleasant conversation might relieve
a dull hour or two.   But if it irks thee,
well, have thy way.   Fergananim, come hither.
See that this young gentleman, my kinsman,
wants for nothing, and, mark you, never come
to him alone or unarmed."

He had an odd assortment of snatches of
songs in many languages.   As he descended
the stone-flight now I heard him hum in
English—

> " Singing so merrily in the dawning of the day—
> And what singest thou, pretty bird, perched on the
> spray ? "

Bridegroom's thoughts, I suppose, recalled,
or possibly created, this snatch of poetry, for

curiously enough Sir Theodore had a native
love for some forms of beauty, in this resembling John Milton's devils, who went apart
from the rest to compose poems and strike
the lyre.

In these settled times it may be a cause of
wonder how the Barretts had the audacity to
undertake a plot so desperate.   But in the
immense confusion of all things, civil and
political, which prevailed just after the overthrow of the Jacobite cause in Ireland, men
of rank and high connections, armed with the
command of money, and unprincipled enough
to forge documents, in Ireland an exceptional
and almost unknown form of crime—such
men, I say, could dare much.   It was a time,
too, when no one thought of consulting a
young girl's wishes as to marriage.

CHAPTER XIV

LOUD LAMENTATION IN DUN-RANDAL

THAT night, about an hour after dark, an immense disturbance arose in the castle. I heard a clamour of many voices, and amongst them, shrill and dominant, charged with the most furious passion, that of Sir Theodore.

"Lost sight of her, you —— children of laziness, folly, and the devil. Fifty thousand acres of land! Son of God! I shall go mad," amid much other passionate vociferation. There was a scuffle, too. I believe Sir Theodore drew upon his men, but was held back by his sons or his officers.

"Launch every boat, then," he cried. "Search east and west. Bring me back the ——, or as my Saviour lives and reigns I will have your necks wrung—of you Con Mac Costello, and you Garret and Pierce Mac Ferris, and of every man who was in the warding boat."

What a veneer was all his foreign polish,
superficial graces, and plausible manners, acquired in many a court and camp during his
wandering life ! Savage and wild, the original
man survived beneath. I do not exaggerate
when I say that after these furious vocifera-
tions and horrible threatenings and blas-
phemies I heard him lift up his voice and
howl like a dog.

Sheela had escaped. In the growing dusk
she had evaded her guard of honour or surveillance, and the bridegroom was left without
his bride and his acres. How I rejoiced and
laughed that night ! And, indeed, over and
above my heartfelt relief at Sheela's escape,
I was amused too, for truly there was something irresistibly comical in that dismal howling of the disappointed bridegroom. From
my window, which opened towards the west,
I could see the torchlights moving to and fro
over the dark sea, where the questing boats
rowed east and west.

During the next day I heard frequent and
angry altercations amongst my cousins. The
escape of the Lady Sheela de Stanton had,
I suppose, quite disturbed their domestic

arrangements.   Under that family settlement
which they had made after my arrival, the
sons, taking with them the bulk of the treasure,
were to have sailed for Spain, they and their
rapparees, while Sir Theodore started on a
fresh career at home as a great gentleman
of the west of Ireland, uniting in his own
person all the station and consequence of two
of the most famous and historic houses there.
All that was now upset, hence these jars.

No alteration, so far, was made in my own
treatment.   That Sheela and her foster-brother
were together somewhere, or in communication, I believed, and also that they would not
forsake me, but use all efforts possible to
effect my liberation.   By certain signs and
tokens I was aware that my treasure, in
accordance with my own written instructions,
reached Dun-Randal this day.   Domestic
amity, too, seemed restored, my precious
cousins having apparently arrived at some
new, if not so brilliant, mutual arrangement.
The vain search for Sheela was continued all
this day too, but in vain.

As soon as the lame giant had paid me his
last visit for the night, I let down from the

window my loaded clue, and sat patiently, holding the clue in my hand like a fisherman, an image which often occurred to my mind, for I was not without a grim sense of the humour of the situation. Yet what I fished for was life—life and also, perhaps, love.

The night was not dark. Three-quarters full, the moon crossed my window about two o'clock, sometimes bright, at times hidden, at times floundering wildly through fleecy clouds. So for hours and hours I sat expectant with my precious clue, Sheela's clue, in my hands, fishing for life, for life, and also for love, hoping, hoping, entertaining, as it were, one ray of golden possibility in a black universe of despair. The transport ship was overdue. As soon as she arrived there would be embarkation. Then Dun-Randal and myself would cease to be. It might have been five of the clock—I could only judge by a guess—when I felt a strong, steady, and unmistakable pull from without at my clue. With a beating heart I drew and drew. Would my thread never come to an end? Then I was aware of some obstruction, which, being overcome, I discovered, a second or two later, that not thread, but cord was now passing through my hands. At last something metallic scraped against the sill. I stood up on the table and secured it. It was a file, to which was attached a little roll of paper. I disengaged the paper, and thrust it into the surest place of concealment that I could discover, rolled up the thread and retained that in my possession, but flung back the cord through the window. I feared that its bulk might lead to a discovery.

Now very gently I began to file through my chains. Gentle, however, as was the motion of my hands, the noise of that abrasion sounded like a shrill screeching in the silence of the sleeping castle. Eventually I hit upon a plan which effectually dulled the noise. I muffled my hands and chains in the woollen rug upon my bed, and so wrought with sounds almost inaudible. Before the day had fully come I was aware that with a very little more exertion on my part I was a free man, so far as my irons were concerned. I did not sleep at all this night. As soon as it was sufficiently light I drew forth the little script and read ; truth to say, I drew it out several times before I could read it. It read as follows :—

"Be prepared to escape to-morrow night, one hour before the turn of the tide."

The writing was uncial, therefore feminine, but though uncial, free, bold, and forceful.

There was no more than this, but it was enough. If my fiendish cousins did not proceed to extremities this day, they would not see me again. I filled the gashes in my handlocks with dust and grease, the little file I thrust into my hair along the crown of my head. The "nameless" one, granite-faced as usual, brought me my breakfast. He wore a sword and pistols, and was attended by an armed soldier. To-day, Fergananim got on to the table and shook the window-stanchion, which, luckily, I had not yet touched, inspected my chains, while my heart stood still for fear ; saw how the handlocks fitted at the wrists, and the footlocks at the ankles, and finally withdrew. Very early Sir Theodore and his sons left the castle. I believe immense marine searchings took place this day, land searchings also, extending far to east and far to west, and all in vain. Working with extreme caution, and with muffled hands, I this day filed through the window stanchion in two places, viz., at the top and bottom, taking care, however, to leave at the lower end a sufficiency of iron to just hold a rope; after that I filled in the abrasions carefully with dust and grease. When Fergananim reappeared with my evening meal, I believe my heart did not beat during the greater part of the time he was in the room. Now, for the first time, I observed in the countenance of that iron man some symptoms of human feeling, some relaxation of the hard and dour visage. He delayed longer than was necessary, thumping round the room, and affecting to set things in order. At last he spoke—

"I crave your pardon, *dhinna oosal*" (gentleman), he said; "'twas I that struck you."

I nodded.

"Sir, one rule is with me since I could speak. It is to obey the master and ask no questions, but right or wrong, good or bad, to do what my master tells me, and that same, sir, is the rudder of my ship. Without it I'd be lost. *Dhinna oosal*, it is your pardon I want."

I gave it him very willingly, both for the blow, and anything else that he might have to do, poor unreasoning tool of a ruffian, and the more willingly because I was so anxious to see his back.

Fergananim's manner was such I perceived that my end, so far as the intentions of my captors was concerned, was now very near.

At last, to my inexpressible relief, he left me, and I was alone.

At night the Barretts with a great company returned to the castle. I heard the noise of much drinking and pledging ; the sounds of revelry did not cease till a late hour. Contrary to my expectation, I heard no noise of any departure. Apparently my cousins, fearing an attack from some quarter, or I know not why, had received a strong ward of their rapparees into the castle. Ere the revelry died away I filed through, and even in trying it tore away the stanchion, but replaced it again artificially. My irons, I believed, I could wrench asunder at any moment.

A good while before the turn of the tide (it was ebbing) I let down my loaded clue and stood expectant, but oh ! with what anxious tremors and beatings of the heart, also with what thrills of glad ʳhope and expectation. Sheela herself was perhaps at this moment beneath my window.

I had not long to wait. Again I felt the steady pull, and drew. After the thread came cord, as before, and after the cord a rope. I mounted the table, knotted the rope to the remnant of the stanchion, and forced myself with difficulty through the narrow window. All was silence and moonlight, and the moaning of the tide, and the piping of night-birds. Below me I saw a dark figure pressing close against the basement wall of the castle. I thought it might be her, but I was wrong. And yet she was not far away. Then letting the rope slide between my hands and knees, after a long descent I reached the ground, and felt the soft sand under my feet. During my descent, though I endeavoured to avoid it, I had been for a moment in front of a lighted window, and had heard some one within there shout fierce interrogations as I slid past. I did not recognise the voice. Some one stood beside me when I reached the ground. I knew him at a glance. It was Conahar MacArdell.

K

Simultaneously I heard a rushing noise. It was my rope falling to the ground. Released from my weight, it had somehow become disengaged from the stanchion-end to which I had attached it. Perhaps the knot slipped. At all events it fell ; and though I hardly noticed it at the moment, I had afterwards abundant reason to be thankful that I had not left behind me this mode of exit out of Dun-Randal.

CHAPTER XV

FLIGHT AND PURSUIT

" FOLLOW me, sir," whispered MacArdell. Just then I heard voices within the castle, and the sound of hurrying feet, fierce interrogations and imprecations, anon the sound of a horn blown from the battlements. My flight had been discovered.

"Run crooked, sir, like myself," cried Conahar, "for they'll have a shot at us."

He was running seaward as he said this, not in a straight line, but slightly zigzag. Almost as he spoke a ball whistled past. Then the shots came fast and furious. To judge by the reports, nearly all the garrison were firing ; but it is not easy to hit a moving object at night, be the moonlight as bright as it may. It was bright moonlight to-night. Before us, on the sea's white verge, clear against the moonlit waters, I saw a dark, slight figure. It was Sheela. In another moment I was by her side.

"Quick, Conahar," she cried, "they are coming."

A curragh lay beside her in the surf.   Conahar, lifting the boat as if it were a feather, ran out into the sea, and flinging it into the water, hastened shorewards, and with incredible speed raced along the edge of the frothing waves towards the west.   As soon as we were embarked, and the curragh in motion under the impulse of Sheela's skilful oarage, I looked round.

"They're in pursuit of Conahar," I said.   " I fear they'll overtake him."

In fact the pursuers had the string of the bow upon him, so to speak, for while they ran straight, he had to run with a curve in order to get round a tongue of sea which went inland some furlongs on the western side of the strand.   Sheela only smiled.   A little after I saw the spray sparkling in the moonlight, where Conahar, with his light feet, dashed across the creek far ahead of his hunters.   We, too, at the same time were flying westward, in the same direction as Conahar.   In another moment we had rounded the rocky spit which formed the western mearing of the sands, and our curragh was scraping against the pebbles of that little beach whence from the battlements I had seen Sheela row forth more than once on her solitary excursions.

"Stave in the boats here," she cried. I sprang ashore, and with pebbles chosen out of the shingle was fulfilling her orders when Conahar joined me. Together we worked at this task, which was by no means an easy one, for the boats were strong and thick-timbered. Before our work was half done I heard Sheela cry to us to desist, and at the same time voices and the trampling of many feet at the strand's head. The pursuers from the castle, fearing an ambush, seemed to have waited till they were joined by their comrades from the town. I hastened to the curragh. One or two shots were fired at us, but in less than a minute we were out of range. I thought Conahar would surely be captured here, for the little strand was almost girt by cliffs, and the enemy held the entrance and the approaches eastward, coming on in momentarily increasing numbers.

As I looked, I seemed to see something grey flitting to and fro along the dark face

of those seemingly perpendicular cliffs lying
to the west of the strand. Then for a few
moments Conahar's athletic form showed
upon the summit dark against the northern
stars. There, regardless of the shots made
at him from the beach, he waved his cap in
bravado, shouted a wild hurroo, and plunging
down somewhere, disappeared from sight. Of
the boats upon the strand, three at least were
still seaworthy. These were now rushed
down into the sea, their keels roaring against
the shingle with a sound which in the stillness
of the night resembled thunder. As the oars
were being run out from the gunwales, I heard
the strident tones of my cousin Enoch shout-
ing commands there. Contrary to my expectation these rapparees seemed expert at rowing,
coast men no doubt before they had enlisted
in the army of King James. That these boats
would speedily overtake a little curragh rowed
by a young girl with a pair of paddles seemed
certain. I myself could give no assistance.
In fact I was a mere passenger, and most
dismally conscious of the fact. And yet in
Sheela's bright watchful eyes and considerate
brow I read a purpose and resolution incon-

sistent with the thought that she expected to
be swiftly overtaken and captured. She first
rowed straight seaward, and in the direction
of that long island which I described in the
first chapter, and the name of which was Lan
Bran. Suddenly she backed with the left
hand, pulled with the right, and doubled the
point of that promontory, up whose cliffs,
where they impended over the strand, I had
just seen Conahar climb like a goat. Doubling
the point she rowed swiftly along its western
side, hugging the rocks, and in a moment shot
out of the moonlight into thick darkness,
where I could not see her, could not even
see my hand.

In the silence that ensued I could hear
the drip of her oars, and the hollow noises
made by the unresting tide in deep cavernous
interiors far beyond ; also the clamour of the
pursuers, and the straining of their oars in
the rowlocks.

Then a black boat, going at a furious pace,
shot past the point, but suddenly making a
wide curve came straight towards us, almost
as if we had been full in the steersman's eye.
Yet that was impossible.

"A noble to a groat they are here, and we have them," I heard him cry.

"Give way there, lads, and if any one has a flint and tinder, rig up something to see by. They never passed the next point."

In a few seconds a light was kindled, and a torch flaring at the bow. The two other boats now showed in the moonlight, but rowed straight forward for the next point. The single boat with which we had to deal was now very close. A large man stood in the bow holding the torchlight. He had long yellow hair, and a red beard and moustache. His comrades called him "Manus." The steersman, who also stood, was a mere lad, a tall, loose-jointed, handsome youth, with a long face, large black eyes, and high and pronounced features. I noticed him particularly, being attracted by his picturesque appearance, and the penetrating quality of his ringing and resonant voice. Sheela, I suppose, guided the curragh just a little out of their track. At all events, the glare of the torchlight as the boat passed did not reach the curragh. We lay seemingly in the wide mouth of a long cavern. The red, smoky torch, the faces, the quivering water-floor, the illuminated points of rock, and the gliding boat, formed altogether a most weird and curious spectacle. Waiting till the boat was partly concealed from sight by some rocky projection, Sheela again dipped her oars and shot straight out into the moonlight, this time, too, straight for Lan Bran. I surmised now that our haven of refuge must be somewhere in that fish-shaped island.

Never a word passed my lips. I knew that the whole soul of the brave and beautiful creature who had charged herself with achieving my salvation was working at the straining height of tension. Why embarrass her with a single question or remark? I was nought here, could do nothing, suggest nothing, and was most miserably conscious of myself as mere weight and clogging encumbrance.

To my surprise at this moment I heard Sheela laugh.

"Prithee, why so sad?" she said, quoting an old song; "but I know. Nevertheless, be not cast down. You shall have a man's work to do presently."

Thus challenged, I made as gay a reply as

possible, and begged to know her purpose, but she would not tell me.

" I shall keep it as a surprise," she said.

Just then I was made aware by shouts from behind that our flight seaward had been discovered, as was but natural when any speck on the moonlit sea was visible for miles around. Looking back, I saw all three boats now beyond the shadows of the cliffs, and straining after us, like greyhounds after a hare, the boat with the torchflare leading considerably. But the flare was now as useless as a candle at noonday, and presently was cast aside. If now but one blessed cloud would cross the moon's track, who could find us on that waste of Atlantic waters ? Vain wish. Cynthia continued to shine nearly full, and a little to the north-west of her zenith.

Sheela still rowed as if she had but just commenced. Though not two feet from that brave and gentle heart, I could not distinguish any quickening of the breath or the faintest inspiration or suspiration. Truly she was a daughter of the sea, as I was the dull son of the fat glebe of the loamy midlands. Now in the moonlight I saw her beautiful countenance as she gazed on our pursuers, pursuers, too, who gained upon us at every stroke, and saw that face bright and beaming, as with a sense of approaching triumph.   Just beyond us, black sided, streaked with green and gold on the back, lay Lan Bran, like a great fish swimming eastwards. What shelter or relief did Lan Bran suggest ? and beyond Lan Bran lay outstretched the illimitable Atlantic without a wave, shining like silver, while almost overhead the moon beamed effulgent, with never a cloud. Yet, my peerless one, she laughed ; she shook back from her face her radiant tresses. She had been in alarm. I had seen it when she doubled that point, and rowed into that sheltering darkness. She was not in alarm now. She did not, I observed, row straight for the island, but for its eastern extremity. What was her purpose ?

CHAPTER XVI

A RED STAR IN THE GLOOM

LOOKING back again, I saw that the boat which had all but lighted upon us in that cave was still far in advance of the others. Sheela now doubled the eastern point of the island, and, slackening her pace, rowed in a leisurely manner along its southern shore. I thought I understood her purpose. She will lead the three boats after us in the same track, and then double back to the mainland in the desperate hope that we might be able to disembark before we are overtaken. Yet, then, why row in this leisurely manner? But I knew nothing. Sheela, rowing along the south side of Lan Bran, suspended her dripping oars at the western extremity of the island till that foremost boat came into view, then she swiftly doubled a long, low spit, which the island cast out here—in fact, one fork of the tail of the whale-shaped island—

literally doubled it, and rowed along its northern side.

Here Lan Bran, true to its fish-like character, extended two points like a divided tail towards the west. Between these Sheela now rowed, moving towards their junction in the body of the island. Before me at that junction rose a black and ragged cliff. Nought else could I see but cliff, though I scanned it with my best eyesight. Yet into this *cul de sac* the girl paddled, rowing now swiftly, indeed, but wearing still that look which seemed to indicate a purpose accomplished. Then in a moment we were once again in dense darkness. Hitherto, I had almost believed that escape was impossible. Though I had the sword which Conahar at parting had thrust into my hands, I felt myself miserably *hors de combat*. In this little rolling boat of skins I could not trust myself to stand, much less to fight. With three well-manned boats in pursuit of our small curragh, rowed by one who was little more than a child, I believed that our capture was only a question of time. Death, I knew, awaited me ; what fate the Lady Sheela de Stanton, I shuddered to think.

Now as we shot seemingly through the sheer, bare, black cliff into the utter darkness, I felt that here, if I could once stand anywhere upon solid ground, instead of this rocking, quivering cradle of scantlings and leather, and have some light by which to see, I might wield a soldier's blade with some effect upon the pursuing crew of rapparees, separated as they were from their companions.

So far as I could guess in that absolute darkness, Sheela seemed to be drawing the little skiff forwards with her hands, for I heard no dip of oars, yet felt that the curragh was moving. I could hear her gunwale crackling from time to time against the sides of the cave, and presently, owing to the echoes so aroused, perceived that, notwithstanding its low and almost unnoticeable entrance, we were now in some cavern of vast dimensions.

Then Sheela broke silence. "The boat just behind us," she said, "is manned by O'Mallys from the Western Isles. We cannot throw *them* off the track. They will follow us hither. You are to do now exactly what I tell you—exactly."

When I expressed my entire willingness, she asked me for my hands, and when she had gained them, which was not easy in the darkness, guided them to what seemed to be a crack in the rock-wall of the cave.

"Hold the curragh here," she said, "until I give my next order."

I knew that she had left the curragh, but held on as directed. Half a minute later I was aware of a light kindled somewhere. I looked upwards, and there at a considerable distance above me stood Sheela, torch in hand, like an apparition, the whole picture framed in darkness.

"Drive the curragh onward strongly and come to me," she cried.

I got on to the rock, and with my left hand launched the skiff onward into the interior, where I heard it strike against gravel. Then I clambered up the rock-wall along the course of that crack, in which, however, I soon perceived that at intervals small footholds had been cut. Sheela held the torch so as to illuminate the ascent. I found her standing on a sort of rocky ledge or shelf some three feet wide, which ran to right and left along the southern side of the cave, and seemed to lie about midway between the water and the roof. I was aware of all this, in a manner unconsciously, for at the moment I was all intent only to hear her instructions and fulfil them ; for I perceived very clearly that I had no clue myself to the puzzles and problems suggested by this cave, which seemed to be so familiar to her.

" Do you see the cave's mouth ? " she said.

I did. It was coal-black in the midst of faintly illuminated rocks.

"Above the lintel," she said, "there is a place on which you can stand. This ledge leads to it. There are pebbles there. Take one and drop it into the first boat that enters."

Something resembling a rude path, in fact, the continuation of the ledge, seemed to lead from the spot where we stood to that which she indicated. I made my way thither, and found, right over the cave's mouth, a level platform, and upon it a heap of great smooth pebbles, arranged in a pyramidal shape like cannon-balls. Seizing one of the largest, I stood expectant, holding it in both hands.

Beneath my feet the water-floor quivered and gleamed. Sheela stood perfectly steady in the spot where I left her, steady as a marble statue, torch in hand, her white hand shining on the black stem of the torch, the face, the whole figure framed and set in darkness—a memorable sight. I but cast a glance that way, my attention being fixed on the water below. Now I heard a muffled sound of human voices, and a moment afterwards the black bow of a boat appeared through the cave's mouth, and wedged its way into the faintly glimmering water. There were men standing in her looking forward and rowing as they stood.

"Blessings on them any way," said a voice "to be giving us light to catch them by."

The speaker was that great man whom I had heard formerly addressed as "Manus." Just then another voice, sharp, clear, and resonant, no doubt the steersman's, cried, "Back! back! back! if you value your lives."

The men did back, but it was too late. Half the boat was now in full view.

Slowly I raised the great pebble above my head in both hands, and taking a deliberate

L

aim, so as to avoid striking any of the crew, dashed it downwards with all my force. The boat's strong sheathings and ribs yielded like glass before the impulse of the stone. Simultaneously I saw a red star shoot through the cavern and fall hissing in the water, and all was darkness, but *not* silence, for the wild despairing howl which now rang through the great cave is in my ears as I write, and the smothered cries and gaspings, less loud, yet more horrible, which succeeded. I cannot say I was much affected by the horror of all this at the time. The destruction of these people by me was an act of war, and I suppose Sheela's cause and my own were as righteous as any for which men ever slew or were slain. There was little chance of escape even for a swimmer, for the sides of the cavern were sheer.

Silence now succeeded, broken only by the sinister noises made by the lapping of the tide and strange echoes sounding in the remotenesses of the vast and dark cavern.

CHAPTER XVII

THE KING'S PARLOUR

PRESENTLY I heard the noise of stricken flint and steel, and a second fainter light was kindled, evidently by Sheela. I made my way towards it, scrambling along that rough ledge which I had recently traversed. I now saw Sheela, with a candle in her hand, standing on the ledge indeed, but also in what seemed to be the entrance of a small but furnished, and even sumptuously furnished, chamber. Hangings and draperies and other upholstery I distinctly noticed, not, as may be imagined, without astonishment. This chamber or grotto, which suggested a scene in the "Arabian Nights' Entertainment," opened upon the ledge near the spot where she had formerly stood holding the torch.

I suppose I had paused with an air of amazement, for she smiled and said, " Do not fear. I am no witch. You shall know all presently. You are safe now," she added. "The other boats have gone off shorewards, questing for us in vain. Moreover, the door of this cave is open only at low water. The tide is flowing, and the entrance is now barred. This is 'The King's Parlour.'" So saying, she led the way into the interior. "You are my king now, Sir Untrustful."

It was raillery no doubt, but such raillery! I, her king! I! who was not worthy to kiss the ground before her sacred feet.

"A hero should repose himself, and rest after the achievement of great and arduous labours," she said, laughing lightly, and pointing at the same time to a couch, on which lay a rich coverlet.

"I think it is the heroine who has laboured on this occasion," I replied. "The hero only dropped a stone, as a churl might."

"Do you wish me to pay compliments?" she retorted. "But sit you down. Heroes, I tell you too, sir, cannot do heroic deeds without abundant and nutritious fare. I must not starve my champion."

So saying, she kindled the fuel in a low three-footed brasier. It blazed up at once.

Retreating now behind a curtain, she came again forward in more succinct attire, and armed with a frying-pan, her eyes aglow with housewifely pride and purpose, brandished the same merrily, and commenced her culinary labours, while I could only stare and wonder at this surprising transformation of my divinity, at the perfect naturalness, ease, and grace of her motions while she played this unexpected part, and the very evident pleasure and delight which she took in a task so humble.

"All this grandeur and vain-glory, Sir Knight," she said, waving a disengaged hand round the grotto, "was not intended for you, sir, but for the King. The King! Yet I don't regret the exchange. You did not run away and bid your army keep fighting. I am the army." Here she laughed merrily. "No, I think you would not be clever enough even to imagine a move so prudent. And so you were charmed with your beautiful cousins, and would not accept a warning from a simple rustic maiden. Tell me now how illumination at last came?"

When, in my narrative, I arrived at that final scene with my cousins she grew pale and shivered, but in a moment recovered herself, and her raillery broke out afresh.

"And so you would have drawn single-handed on the whole ward.   Oh! thou art surely a most wise and prudent as well as valiant knight."

Presently she had a little table invitingly spread, and the viands neatly dished, and with mock humility and the profoundest of curtseys, begged " My valour to sit and eat."   She would not sit herself.   " I am a lowly damsel," she said, "and must wait upon my knight."

"And what now will your valour choose to drink ?   Remember I have a king's cellar here."

As for myself, rapt in the seventh heaven of bliss, I knew not what I ate or drank.   Her gentle raillery played around me all the time; indeed, she seemed to glance over, through, and about me with the swift ease of some bright bird upon the wing, and to feel some unaccountable delight in the slower and more cumbrous movements of my own plain understanding.

"Inquisitiveness does not seem to be one of your foibles," she said presently ; "you have not asked one single question concerning this brilliant and well-stored chamber, found in the heart of Lan Bran."

Now, literally for the first time I forced my eyes to wander from the owner of this fairy grot. That former impression of splendour had been produced mainly by a very brilliant arras of hanging and folded curtains, by which bare rock walls were draped, save where there was, on one side, a row of shelves containing a miscellaneous assortment of things, including weapons, and even some books.

"Chivalry tales," she said, in reply to my look. "Madame La Faure had them sent to me all the way from Rochelle. Raymond and I——"

Here she paused; all the gay light died suddenly in her eyes, all the colour left her cheek.

"Oh, I had forgotten it all, forgotten it all. Selfish! Selfish! because I am myself so hap——"

I started up, and kneeling before her said passionately—

"Lady Sheela de Stanton, I swear to you, as I am a Christian and a gentleman, that I shall not leave this country without doing all that one man may, perilling his life to the utmost, and losing it if necessary, so I may compel those fiends to surrender your dear brother whole and unscathed. And I swear, too, that if he has met, or shall meet, with ill at their hand, I shall devote my life to the task of exacting a full vengeance upon those miscreants, pursuing them even to the ends of the earth. This my life is no longer mine, but yours, since you saved it." I believe that I would have gone on there and then to avow my love had I not perceived that she was weeping.

After a few minutes' silence she spoke again. " I accept your offer," she said, looking at me more gently than ever before. "I do believe that a few brave men may yet save the Baron, my brother, alive out of their hands. Such a band my foster-brother, whose fidelity to me the Barretts did not suspect, so prudent has been his bearing towards them, has been organising amongst his friends and my own loyal tenants. He tells me, however, that I must show myself to them, so that they may know that they are acting under my authority. Our plan is to seize Sir Theodore himself, and having him as a hostage, compel the sons to deliver up my brother. That he is still alive I know. He is in irons, in darkness, confined in some unknown prison. So much I know, but how I know it must remain my secret. Now, to take Sir Theodore at the head of his men is impossible; but there is a subterranean entrance into Dun-Randal, the secret of which is known only to one person in the world. That person is Conahar's grandmother, who was nurse to my father's father, and she is under a solemn vow to reveal it only to my brother, and to him only when he comes of age. If, however, I could see and talk with her, if I could convince her that the Baron is their prisoner, and in peril of his life, I believe that she would reveal it to me. For both these purposes I go ashore at the next falling of the tide. If all goes well we shall arrange the time and mode of the attack, and you shall lead the storming party. Is your valour satisfied now? I see you are burning to do some great deed."

Of course I expressed my glad willingness, but added, "You will be in peril going ashore.

Might not a letter from myself to the Governor of the Province be more effective ? The King's troops would be around Dun-Randal in a few days."

"But the Spanish transport might be here to-morrow," she replied, "and in the movement of State armies there are always difficulties and delays."

"Let me go ashore with you then," I implored.

"Nay, nay," she said resolutely. "There are many reasons why you should not ;" adding with some touch of her former raillery, "alone I can shoot about almost anywhere in my little curragh, flitting like a sea-gull through the intricacies of this crannied and rocky coast. I could row everywhere here in the dark, but not with a man of war like you, sir, a great-limbed martialist, and—and—" she laughed as she discharged this shaft—"a passenger. Let us go on as we have begun. I am the clear, directing intelligence, you are the strong, executive right hand."

"Yet," said I, "I think it is to your hands as much as to your wisdom that I owe my salvation."

"Nay, sir, contradict me not, I am head, you are hand."

Afterwards, growing more serious, she imparted to me a great deal of recondite family history concerning the past relations of the de Stanton and Barrett families, too recondite, and of an interest too indirect and secondary to that of my tale, to be set down in writing.

"Sir Theodore and his sons," she said, "from the moment of their arrival in Dun-Randal, gained a great ascendency over the mind of my brother. He was young, home-bred, bright, sanguine, and trustful; they experienced soldiers and men who had seen the world. I warned him against them as I did your proud and unbelieving self, but in vain. At first I simply disliked and distrusted them; but one day, shortly before they left for Limerick, I had a singular experience. All your cousins were in a room surrounding my brother, and making much of him, as their manner was. As I entered a strange feeling came over me, so that for a few moments all five seemed to me like figures in a dream, and their voices sounded far off; also I was aware of

an inexpressible loathing and abhorrence
of these men. Then suddenly I seemed
to see all four stripped of those outward
and accidental gifts and graces, and the men
themselves in their true characters horribly
revealed."

Here she shuddered, and was silent.

"What my guardian angel caused me then
to see," she added, "I may not, nay, I cannot, express in words. When I told this experience to my brother he only laughed as
at a girlish freak or fancy. He was young,
sanguine, and high-spirited, and could think
evil of no one. So he marched off to Limerick
with the Barretts, his heart full of hope and joyful anticipation of the war. This was all after
the defeat at Aughrim. Some months afterwards Sir Theodore and his two younger sons
returned, attended with a crowd of rapparees,
the dregs of that bad army which followed
Baldearg O'Donnell plundering through Connaught. He told me that my brother had
sailed for Spain, and brought me a document
under my brother's hand directing him to
assume possession of our treasure and plate,
and the control and management of his estates,

and also directing me to obey him as my guardian and protector. I believe it was forged. Afterwards Lord ——, acting for Sir Theodore, showed me another document subscribed in the same manner. You remember how he bellowed and roared. It was on the same day that I escaped from Dun-Randal." She covered her face with her hands as she said this, and sobbed out, "Oh, they are wicked, wicked, wicked, past all telling."

I did not say a word ; I knew too well what that document contained.

"You have not yet explained to me," I said, in order to divert her thoughts, "the secret of this wonderful place which you call 'The King's Parlour.'"

She responded with unexpected animation, "My brother Raymond and myself discovered this great cave when we were children. Its existence is a secret even from the fisher people of the coast, for its mouth is only exposed at low water, and the entrance gives no promise of this noble cave. Even then we determined that if ever we or any of our friends were in peril, this, which is the most perfect of hiding-places, we would make our

retreat and stronghold.   This little grotto, or
rock parlour, in which we now sit is as we
found it, save for all these furnishings and
embellishments, and some chiselling along the
walls for shelves.   The great outer ledge,
which runs along this side of the cave, we
widened and levelled — that is to say, my
brother and Conahar did, for we took Conahar into the secret.   Two men could maintain
the cave against an army, for there is fresh
water here, too.   There is a little stream and
well of the purest water in a recess at the
inner end, just above the shingle.   The boys
hewed out the well in the rock there.   Indeed,
they did a great deal of hewing, cutting, and
carving here in these old happy days while
I was their housewife.   This grotto was then
called 'Sheela's Kitchen.'   When, by levelling
the ledge, they had made a road from my
kitchen to a point just above the cave's mouth,
they contrived a sort of platform there, and
brought thither that pyramid of pebbles—you
now know why.   Every summer, in calm
weather, we spent much time here, always
keeping the place a perfect secret.   Well,
when, two years since (we were a great deal

younger then than we are now), the Civil War
first broke out, our minds being full of tales
of the romantic escapes of the Second Charles
after the battle of Worcester, we conceived
the idea of King James flying to us for refuge
after some similar disaster ; so we laboured
industriously to render this a fit spot for
the temporary lodgment of Majesty, and re-
christened 'Sheela's Kitchen' as 'The King's
Parlour.' Hence all this splendour of arras,
hangings, and gay upholstery.

"Madame La Faure, whom Sir Nicholas
sent to me, was with us then, and was let into
the secret. She is as romantic as a school-
girl, the dearest and sweetest lady in the
world. It was she who made me so charming
and accomplished—why do you not bow, sir,
and lay your hand upon your heart ?—and
taught me to love tales of chivalry. Even
down to the coming of the Barretts, Raymond
was boy enough to take delight in this fancy,
and after he and they went to Limerick, I
myself from time to time brought hither
various articles of use, luxury, or convenience.
Such was my distrust of Sir Theodore, that
now, in all seriousness, I believed that some

time it might be necessary, even for myself, to retain such a stronghold and retreat."

" I fear," said I, with the air of an experienced soldier, "that the defence of this stronghold might be neutralised."

" How ? "

" By smoke."

" Explain," she said, but with laughing eyes.

" The enemy," I replied, " bring in a boat laden with straw, or some other combustible material, and fire it. Those who make caves their stronghold are always dealt with so, and suffocated, or compelled to go out."

" O distrustful knight ! I shall convince you that even in Connaught there is just a little military knowledge, and a ray, or perhaps two, of intelligence. Follow me."

She drew aside a curtain which draped the inner end of our grotto and went on, candle in hand, through a chamber filled with many and divers stores, quite a magazine on a small scale. At a certain point she held the candle close to the rock wall of the cavern. The flame blew sidewise. She went to a different point, and did the same, with a like result.

" Yes," I said, with intense joy, for the

blown candle flame dissipated a horrible fear
which had begun to fill me. "The boys," I
said, "have drilled vent-holes in the cavern.
You were the clear, directing intelligence;
they the strong, executive right hands."

"Yes," she replied. "Fortunately we found
by calculation that between us and the outer
surface the distance was small. The boys,
too, lessened that by quarrying and blasting.
The rock there, on the outside, where those
vent-holes open, is now concealed with vegetation. Were we not clever? If the enemy
seek to smoke us out, we just seal up the
entrance of 'The King's Parlour.' All that is
necessary for that purpose is here. So the
defenders live, breathe, and are happy while
the great cavern outside is filled with smoke.
Meantime, as they believe that we are dead,
they leave themselves open to terrible re-
prisals at our hands."

This was said with a charmingly belligerent air and manner. Till I had set myself
down to write these memoirs, I had never
realised how utterly inadequate words are to
describe anything which is not of the plainest
and most prosaic character. I seem to see

M

my darling this moment as I saw her then ;
her pure, clear face, with its brilliant colour-
ing ; the rich auburn hair, and white neck,
lit up in the flickering light of the candle
which she held in her hand ; her outlined,
slender form, the high, saucy, belligerent, and
withal most maidenly air, pose, and manner,
all showing so clearly against the darkness.
Yet to convey all that by written words is as
much beyond my power as to reproduce with
this wretched quill the passion of love and
admiration with which I regarded her.   While
I stood and gazed she broke off suddenly,
and returned to "The King's Parlour."

CHAPTER XVIII

LIEUTENANT LOCHLIN O'MALLY

PRESENTLY Sheela, on household cares intent, left me for a few moments, re-passing the curtain which divided the parlour from the store-chamber of this very well-appointed grotto. Longing for her reappearance, I sat like one entranced, staring at the crimson folds which, for a moment that seemed like an age, concealed her from my sight.

Suddenly there struck upon my ear, amid the other curious noises of the cave, a sound indubitably human. It sounded like a very natural and honest yawn, suddenly breaking off in the middle. I started to my feet. Concerning the reality of this very human sound I could entertain no doubt. It was too ludicrously natural, though certainly it was not its ludicrous character which struck me at the moment. Yes, there was a third person in the cave, and it was a man. Who could he be ? One man certainly, possibly

more than one, had escaped from the foun-
dered boat. Where was he, then ? Almost
certainly on that strand at the extremity of
the cave, whither I had driven forward the
curragh, and where I had heard her keel
scraping against the stones. I determined,
without exciting Sheela's alarm, to proceed
thither and explore. When she reappeared,
I said with such carelessness as I could
assume—

" I think I shall scramble down to that strand,
and make the curragh secure."

" There is no necessity," she said, " but if you
like, do so. You will at least learn the geog-
raphy of this underground world. When you
return, I shall show you your bed-chamber."

She came with me part of the way, and
pointed out where the ledge, which ran past
the grotto and half encircled the cave, trended
downwards towards the beach. She then left
me and returned, happy and even singing.
With a candle in one hand, and my drawn
sword in the other, I made my way over very
rough ground to that strand.

I had scarcely set my foot on the shifting
shingle, when I was aware that I was standing

face to face with a young man, who sat upon
a large stone there, and regarded me with
an easy and nonchalant air.   I recognised
him at once.   It was the same youth who
had so nearly captured us earlier in the night,
the steersman of the leading boat.   His
features, illuminated then by the torchlight,
were very clearly remembered by me.   He
sat now with one leg crossed over the over,
swaying his right foot gently, gently and non-
chalantly, in mid-air, his eyes fixed upon mine
with a comically saucy expression.   While we
so stared at one another, he commenced to
hum a tune.   Suddenly he broke off and said,
but with the air of one who cared little what
answer he received—

" Peace or war ? "

" You came here," I replied, " to capture and
give up to our enemies myself and a lady
who did you no wrong.   If I hold you as a
foe, and send you to join your wicked comrades, no one could charge me with giving
you more than your deserts, though I confess I am loath to add to the number of those
whom I have slain already, and especially a
mere youth like yourself."

The blood mounted to his face, but when I looked to see him start to his feet, he only stirred a little and sat still.

"You talk," he replied, "of killing an armed man, as a butcher might of killing a pig. I have met your betters, proud gentleman, and they did not ride or walk from the place of meeting. No one who knows Lochlin O'Mally will think it is from fear that he once again says, 'Peace or War?' for indeed I mind your bit of steel no more than that," making as he said so a certain gesture, which I think I had better not write down. "If I had held you as an enemy," he went on, "and if I were not a gentleman, I could have just now put my sword through you before you could have said 'bah,' for on rocky ground your motions are not those of a goat. And let me tell you, that had you come within my reach an hour since, you would have fared badly, for I had five deaths of good soldiers, my own men, to avenge, and I had not yet considered the other, your side of the argument. But how say you? It comes to my mind that this question of peace or war might be more profitably and wisely debated over a flask of Rhenish or Canary, and by a pleasant fire. St. Mullish, that was a joyous report which rang through the cavern when you drew cork, and that an agreeable odour of bacon which just now floated this way. And indeed, I was on my way up to open negotiations, when you elected rather to submit yourself to my mercy. And I can tell you, that it is no agreeable pastime sitting in wet clothes in the dark, with an empty stomach for company and a dry throat, listening to the sounds of revelry and the report of drawn corks, and the agreeable conversation of coevals. Therefore, Lieutenant Netterville, delay not."

All this was said with an air of invincible good-humour. There was something arch and comical in the youth, which utterly precluded the possibility of deadly combat between us.

"I believe," I said, "that you are one whose word may be trusted. Tell me, then, how I find you in the company of those abandoned, bloody, and treacherous villains, the Barretts?"

"Why, lieutenant," he retorted, "but a few days since one might have put to you exactly that same awkward question. Did I not find you in the very bosom of the Barretts?"

As I did not reply to this well-planted retort, he went on—

"I came hither but ere yesterday, seeking passage to the Groyne. When you were captive and put in irons they told us you were a Williamite spy and other things, and when the alarm was sounded I merely rose up and pursued. And mind," he said, "I do not make this explanation out of fear, but in the courtesy that one gentleman owes to another, and truly also for the expediting of terms of peace, and the speedier satisfaction of certain desires not to be endured, for it was before supper that the bugle sang in Dun-Randal."

"You seem a whimsical young gentleman," I replied, "yet I think you are to be trusted. Give me your sword, and you have my peace for the present. Make your peace now with the Lady Sheela de Stanton, and I shall restore it."

He sprang up at once with alacrity, unbuckled and put his sword in my hand, and snatching the candle clomb the rocky ascent, I following, *non passibus æquis.*

Sheela, who had overheard the whole colloquy, was now seated somewhat *en grande dame* in the grotto. She received the youth with much graciousness, and an evident pleasure, which for a moment sent a pang through my jealous heart. Lochlin, on the other hand, who I feared might prove noisy and familiar, behaved to her with the profoundest deference and respect, and showed in his whole manner and bearing that at least the social side of his education had not been neglected. Sheela now, seemingly with abundant pleasure, prepared supper for our hungry guest, whose eyes were, I noticed, fixed the whole time upon the bubbling and frizzling viands, a fact which gave my anxious mind relief, for, as I have said, the youth, though somewhat lanky and loose-jointed, was very handsome.

There is always a pleasure in seeing hungry animals being fed, and this pleasure was ours while Lochlin was despatching the decidedly large supply of food which had been prepared for him. Then I drew for him a bottle of wine which Sheela produced, and again the report rang echoing through the wild cavern.

"When I heard that noise before," he re-marked, "I can assure you it was not so agreeable to the ear."

Then he turned suddenly on me.

"I wish I had seen you," he said, "before they put you in irons."

"Why?"

"You don't look like a spy. They told us you were that, a Williamite spy. Though, indeed, there was a time when I firmly be-lieved that no Williamite could be an honest man."

"Do you know why they put me in irons?" I said.

"No, though I partly guess," he said, with a demure look, and a faint suspicion of a smile. He looked at Sheela as he spoke. She, poor child, was quite ignorant of his meaning.

"It is not as you suppose," I said.

I then proceeded to give him a full account of all the abominable knavishness practised upon me by Sir Theodore and his sons, an account punctuated by many a fierce and indignant comment from him.

"The children of the devil," he cried, when

I had concluded. "From this moment I forswear all service to them. I am your ally from this night, and the Lady Sheela's true servant and follower, to command as she may please. Nay, lady, before this my mind was revolting against them, both on account of themselves and the vile churls whom they have in their pay, and whom they call soldiers, and I kept to myself altogether, and had no share in their doings."

Sheela then told him of her belief that the Baron was still alive, but concealed somewhere under watch and ward. She also communicated to him her plans.

After we had considered all the serious aspects of the affair our talk grew lighter and gayer. Finally, Sheela produced from her inexhaustible treasures a little hand harp in its sheath. Lochlin's eyes glowed again when the instrument was revealed from its covering.

Sheela handed the little harp to Lochlin, who drew back coyly, saying, "Nay, lady, you first with your witching melodies, afterwards your slave."

He bowed nigh to the ground as he said

this. I was amused at his antics, and yet he looked quite sincere.

Unluckily I have myself no ear for music, but to my mind Sheela's singing and playing of the "*Fuam na Thonn*," the "Noise of the Waves," an old song, but said to be very beautiful, was perfect. When she sang, "racing shorewards after rocks break them like white hounds questing," I thought of many a glorious burst in which I had shared with the good gentlemen of Meath, ere these King troubles had arisen to divide us. Other songs, too, she sang, which I do not remember, so much was my attention riveted on her own sweet self. Lochlin, I observed, paid less attention to the singer than to the song.

"And I can match that," he said at last, reaching out his hands for the harp in what struck me as a rather *exigeant* manner. He tuned the strings to his liking, and indeed that seemed no easy task. Then he broke out into a most wild and lamentful ditty, fit to make a man hang himself, all about a certain Kathleen, with a surname which I cannot recall, a lady, as I deemed, of unimpeach-

able behaviour and wondrous beauty, who
had fallen a prey to giants and Turks and all
manner of misconducted sons of perdition.
When he had finished and hung with bowed
head over the little harp, and weeping as I
do believe, I said cheerfully—

"Lieutenant, if the lady be surrounded
with such enemies, and if you have it in
your mind to attempt a rescue, count me
as one of your comrades in the adventure,
always provided that this business now in
hand be seen through to the end."

As I spoke I laid my hand in comrade
fashion on the shoulder of the weeping youth.
He started back in a manner which was
anything but polite, and regarded me one
moment with a proud, high, disdainful, and
yet sorrowful look, his eyes the while flashing through tears which glittered on the
eyelids.

He said nothing, not one word, but looked
at Sheela as if he would say "*you* understand
me," and taking from her hands the doeskin
harp-case, carefully enclosed in it that instrument of melody, after which, kissing the same,
he restored it to the hands of the owner,

and contemplated the embers in the brasier for a long time in silence.

More than once since then I have asked Sheela to tell me what it all meant, but her invariable reply has been, " Nay, you would not understand. We Jacobites have our own mysteries."

.That Kathleen was not the name of his mistress, I afterwards learned from his own lips. Her name was Joan. After a long time spent in a silence which I did not know how to break, Lieutenant O'Mally at last dragged himself up again from that pit into the realm of speech, and truly to no very poetical results.

" Fair lady," he said, " it is a custom with me, derived from my ancestors, to smoke tobacco leaf ere I sleep. Amongst thy various and many commodities stored up here for the use and pleasure of the King and his grooms, hast thou perchance——"

" Surely I have," she replied, smiling. "That, too, did not escape the mind of my dear brother."

From her magazine Sheela now produced the instruments of tobacco fumigation. Lochlin slowly and meditatively filled the pipe which she had brought him. Then as if suddenly waking to consciousness of her presence, he said, "Thou art doubtless weary, flower of the flowers—all save one——"

He looked at me, "The Williamite, doth he perchance—— ?"

"No," said I, laughing, "it hath been no such custom with my ancestors; but I shall bear you company with pleasure while you perform the rite."

We both rose now, intending to pass the rest of the night together on that shingle.

"Did you think that you were to sleep on that cold strand?" said Sheela, the light of hospitality shining in her beautiful eyes. "Nay, I have a good bedchamber ready and furnished in all respects, which you shall both share."

Like a lady doing the honours of her own house, she begged us to stay longer. In such a place it was most strange and wondrous pretty.

Finally she conducted us along the ledge in the direction of the cave's mouth, and on the way paused before a sort of recess or alcove. "This place," she said, smiling, "we had intended for the King's gentlemen. See, here are many things that such great people might need." She showed us a shelf on which were candles in their candlesticks, which she lit, jars containing drink of some description, and cups, on the floor a brasier filled with fuel, which she ignited, and a canvas bag bulging with biscuits. There was also a tub, a jug, and towels hanging from a projection in the rocky wall.

"Now," she said to me, smiling, "while our guest is consuming his tobacco leaf according to the custom of his ancestors, you can explore the contents of these," indicating the jars aforesaid. "After which sweet slumber and agreeable dreams, or none according to your desires."

She then made to withdraw, but we both accompanied her back to the King's chamber, Lochlin going before and bearing the torch ; after which we returned, I more madly in love than ever, Lochlin grateful and admiring indeed, but, to my joy, no more than that.

Well, not to be tedious, Lochlin, for whom I had conceived a great liking, and myself sat up in our alcove for a long time. Our talk was partly about the war, and it surprised me how generously he praised the valour of William at the forcing of the Boyne, of Schomberg the father, and of Schomberg the son, and, in fact, of every one who had done well on the Williamite side. This I say surprised me, for I confess that amongst my own war-comrades I had often deplored a tendency to belittle and decry the valour of our opponents, which was the more ungenerous seeing that we lacked for nothing, while our Jacobite foes were very ill-furnished in all respects, be the cause what it may.

I pass over his duels with renowned swordsmen in that army, for the same have been reported to me differently; and though the youth was brave and apt with his sword, nay, with sword and dagger, and with bombardules, too, I cannot believe that he was altogether so successful as he gave himself out.

Gradually it was borne in on me that this youth, be his faults and follies what they might, had a high exalted and noble spirit, and also truly that he had a wonderful gift of speech. Crouched there in his blanket

N

while we dried his clothes at the brasier, with his long brown face and large dark eyes showing curiously in the flickering light, talk poured abundantly from his lips, an ever-flowing river of speech.   But my own thoughts for the most part were elsewhere.

CHAPTER XIX

SECOND ASSAULT OF THE KING'S PARLOUR

I AWOKE, having slept I knew not how long. First, I was aware of the somewhat sonorous nature of my comrade's mode of culling the sweet flower of sleep. Then I heard the sobbing of the waves, and the strange echoes. A dull red eye stared at me in the darkness. It was an ember half-covered with ashes, which still glowed in the brasier. As I lay awake, listening and watching, I heard the noise of oars and the drip of water. Some one was leaving the cave, and in our curragh.

I started up with a cry of challenge, to which the reply came in tones which were surely a contrast with my strident roar, for I was answered by Sheela. The tide had fallen once again, unbarring our water-gates, and Sheela, as she had promised, was on her way to the mainland, and alone.

"Lady Sheela," I cried, "you must let me accompany you."

"No, no," she said, "it is impossible, and there is no danger at all, for it is the darkest hour of night, the hour before dawn. I shall be back ere the tide flows—back for breakfast! Farewell! And a word more, keep good watch and ward."

All was dark here. I could see nothing, only hear her sweet voice and the strange echoes of it.

I awoke Lochlin, and communicated to him all my doubts and misgivings.

"Nay, be not cast down," he replied cheerfully; "thy lady is wise as well as brave."

"My lady! No more mine than another's," I replied, for his composure, as well as his assumption, nettled me. I thought of all that animated conversation which took place last night between her and this soulless youth, who actually lay snoring while the music of her voice, for perhaps the last time, rang here.

"Lieutenant," he said gently, "I, too, have suffered for love's sweet sake. Love—love unreturned—sends me a roamer and an exile into the wide world. But misery ofttimes softens the heart, and wherever I see true love burn and tremble, there I am a gentle and tender watcher."

I almost laughed at this sentimental exordium, remembering the speaker's supper, and his pipe, and his more recent prosaic performances.

"Trouble thyself no more," he continued, "torment thyself no more. Believe me, true love for thee mounts like a tide in that young heart. Trust me, the observer of many maidens, for I know the tokens of it. Now strike a light, and let us breakfast."

This, however, I would not do, telling him of Sheela's promise to be back for that meal. We then kindled torches, and having nothing else to do, amused ourselves by exploring the cavern.

Its height in the highest place was, as I guessed, about fifty feet; its length, from the entrance to the Baron's well, which we found at the cave's innermost extremity at the head of the shingle, about one hundred and twenty. Truly, as Sheela had promised me, the water in this well was a wonder, clear as crystal,

sweet and refreshing. But the most remark-
able features of the cave were the ledge which
ran half round it on the left side, as one faced
the entrance, and that singular grotto, "The
King's Parlour," opening upon it like a one-
chambered house opening on a street. I have
to mention, however, that it was a little lower
than the ledge. You entered the grotto by
two steps cut in the rock. The alcove, in
which Lochlin and myself passed the night,
was quite artificial, and so I think to a considerable extent was the platform above the
lintel of the cavern door. The whole ledge,
too, showed marks of the boys' hammers and
chisels.

Time passed, and my heart grew anxious.
With a growing alarm I stood, torch in hand,
watching the black mouth of the cavern, how it
slowly disappeared with the inflowing tide. At
last I had to confess, with a feeling akin to
despair, that Sheela's return was no longer to
be expected. Possibly she was safe on shore
under Conahar's protection, but, again, possibly—dreadful thought !—in the possession of
those devils.

Lochlin now prepared breakfast, there where

Sheela with her own beautiful hands had prepared supper for us last night, and, as it
seemed to me, he did so with a certain heart-
less alacrity, though I confess, too, that he
moved about and handled his culinary utensils
like a very clever and experienced cook.

"Eat and drink, O Williamite," he said.
"There may be fighting toward, and nought
is good hollow in the hour of battle save a
drum."

He set me an excellent example, but in
vain.

Both during and after this meal, of which,
however, he seemed to partake with much
relish, he confided to me, with the utmost
particularity and a needless enlargement of
quite unimportant details, his own dismal love
story; and I regret to say that on my side I
had so little of manly pride and self-control
as to unburthen utterly, in his strangely un-
sympathetic ears, my own love-laden heart.
I confess I was amazed to find that this young
gentleman, while assenting readily, so far as
words went, to everything I said, even to the
extent of finding with me some mysterious
correspondence between that flashing star

seen above the black turrets of Dun-Randal and the radiant child of high heaven captived there, did not, as I enlarged on this and other aspects of my astonishing relations with that wondrous being, seem to catch any responsive fire.

To Lochlin, in spite of his dark mysterious eyes and long visage, which at times could look almost preternaturally solemn, the Lady Sheela de Stanton was just a brave and beautiful maiden, and no more. However promising they may appear to the eye, it is extraordinary how barren some natures can be. Apart from his whimsicalities, and when not, as on the shingle, ruffling his war-plumes and erecting his crest, he was polite and urbane to a singular degree, and his "Quite so," and his "Williamite, say no . more," and his frequent hand on the heart, no honest soul could resist.

"Did you remark," I said, "the way she stamped her foot on the ground when she bade me, for the second time, go for water to the Baron's well, while I was rapt in the seventh heaven of her angel face ?"

"*Ma foi*, lieutenant," he said, in his French

style, picked up in the entourage of St. Ruth, and with his hand on his heart the while, "it was inexpressible, it was divine."

Now, no one could quarrel with his language, still less with his behaviour on this occasion, for the manner in which Sheela had taken command of me, as if I were quite her individual property, and the manner in which she enforced her authority, were indeed ineffably charming. Nevertheless I was profoundly aware that my *vis-à-vis* and love-confidant was, at the moment, thinking perhaps of his proud and scornful beauty in the extreme west, Joanna de Costello, or of that unlucky cannon ball which carried off St. Ruth's noble head in the bog of Aughrim, or of Patrick Sarsfield and his very subordinate position in the Jacobite councils, or I know not what; knowing only that his heart did not go with the singularly apposite words which seemed to roll with so much naturalness, nay, sentiment, from his lips on this occasion. Again, when I referred to my beautiful one's "bright blue eyes," he said—

"Pardon me, monsieur, but they are dark grey. You will, I am sure, confess, Lieutenant

Netterville, that blue eyes, much less dark blue eyes, are almost never matched with that complexion of hair."

I confess that, for one moment, I was on the point of giving him the lie direct on the spot, the more so as I was aware that he had not once fairly looked at the Lady Sheela de Stanton, whereas my eyes had been, as it were, anchored on her countenance the whole night.

Extraordinary to relate, however, I have since discovered that this wild son of the Islands was right, and I wrong; another proof, if, at this time of day, it were needed, that love is blind. Love, I strongly opine, is deaf too, for it seems as if I had been twice commanded to go for water ere I went; of one command only am I, or was I then, aware.

Yet, after all, there was no quarrelling with Lieutenant O'Mally. Whether learned from St. Ruth and his officers, or from some uncouth West of Ireland exemplars, dating back, maybe, from the time of the famous Granuaile (Grace O'Mally) or beyond, the youth's manners were such that I would defy the angriest and most captious man in Europe to quarrel with him, feeling that justice and the laws of courtesy were on his side.

Nevertheless, though I could not quarrel with him I felt aggrieved, and spent a good deal of this day pacing to and fro on the ledge by myself, rapt in loving thoughts, also, I confess, in thoughts angry and jealous. My new friend had not praised Sheela as he ought, yet I dare say that even if John Milton, whom I suppose I ought not to admire, but whom I do, were to come to me that night with a poem in praise of the Lady Sheela de Stanton, he could not have praised her so as not to hurt me. And, touching this mighty poet, I am but too well aware that Sheela's imperiousness and high airs of command, which I loved then and love now, but badly accord with the great Puritan's ideal woman—meek "accomplished Eve." And yet, in the matter of "accomplishments," though *I* say it, I believe no woman anywhere approached my Sheela in anything which it is honourable for a woman to know and do. She could draw and paint, she could read and also write, she could speak Irish, English, French, and Italian, and a little Spanish. Madame La Faure had taught her those languages. She knew more Latin than I did; it was all a *ruse de guerre* when she brought me that sentence to be translated. She could spin, sew, knit; she could cook; she could play the part of *la grande dame* in withdrawing-rooms. I never saw a woman enter a room so superbly. She could keep a whole group of men, of the most diverse qualities, engaged in very animated conversation round her chair; she rode fairly well, not very well; she could row a curragh better than any fisherman on the west coast; she could shoot out of a bombardule or matchlock with the best of us; and when alone with one she liked, whether man or woman, she could make six hours pass like one. Therefore, if she was not "accomplished," I do not know what that word may mean. But I am an old fool and twaddler—let me get on.

Later, in the course of my very extensive ruminations, it occurred to me that this youth, Lieutenant Lochlin O'Mally, having broken with the Barretts, and having joined himself with us in our quarrel, might haply be in a somewhat precarious condition as to worldly prospects. I found him reading in " The King's Parlour," and seemingly very much absorbed in his author. He laid his book aside at once the moment I began to confer with him about his own past, present, and future—themes concerning which all men are very willing to enlarge before sympathetic listeners.

From Lieutenant Lochlin O'Mally I now learned that after the break-up at Limerick he had no choice but Sarsfield and France, with transport provided by the Government, or "Spain with Sir Theodore," at his own " proper cost and peril," "and because," he went on, " I have divers well-affectioned kinsfolk in the Spanish service ever since the days of Queen Bess of happy memory, who report very well of the same, I concluded for Spain, though at my proper cost. Had I guineas sufficient I would have chartered a ship of my own, taken out a company of likely soldiers, and so entered the Spanish king's service a full captain. I owe Sir Theodore nothing, not one angel. I paid him nigh my last crown to transport me and my five cousins."

For a moment his face grew stern and his

eye glittered, but the look—it was no pleasant
look—vanished.

"Cousins!" I cried, aghast.

"Well, Connaught cousins," he replied, more
cheerfully; "children of the great Uaill like
myself; from one of the out islands of the
Atlantic. My sergeant enlisted them, and
they came hither on coat and conduct money,
at my charges, indeed, but not in my company. And, indeed, O Williamite, I never
saw them before I came hither, and truly their
cousinship was in no way agreeable to me.
Yet cousins they were."

He gloomed again as he said this. The
obligations of blood were very strong in those
days.

"Lochlin," I said—"permit me to call you
Lochlin—I owe you reparation for that drown-
ing of your men, though my quarrel was just,
and I did it in self-defence. Moreover, I am
your debtor for the service which you have
promised to the lady and myself, and you
shall yet have your chartered ship and your
company if together we carry this adventure
through successfully, and if I recover my
treasure out of that black keep."

O'Mally, no doubt, had intended to serve me and Sheela faithfully from sheer sympathy and sentiments of honour. But hope is a great stimulus to action, and when we had pledged right hands on this contract, I perceived, or thought I perceived, in him a keenness of interest, an alacrity, and a zeal in our quarrel with the Barretts, which were not so noticeable before. To enter the Spanish service as a full captain, commanding a company, was evidently something to which he had often looked forward as the far-off and nigh impossible goal of his ambition in his calling of soldier and man of the sword.

It was about six o'clock in the morning when Sheela left us, consequently the water-gate would not be effectually unbarred till four or five o'clock in the evening of this day. Lochlin, who under other circumstances might have been an entertaining companion, finding that he could not effectually interest me in the things in which he was interested, and that I could not interest him, buried himself again in one of Sheela's romances. It was Madame La Faure who introduced her to this species of literature, and who supplied her with all those chivalry books. O'Mally spent the whole of this day in "The King's Parlour"—nay, upon Sheela's own velvet-lined couch. There sitting, he swayed to and fro reading to himself, and aloud, too, whenever some particularly beautiful passage struck his fancy. Indeed, I may say that he forgot everything in his selfish absorption.

At length this long and mournful day drew towards evening, and the black entrance began to disclose itself, out of whose blackness I soon began to look for the emergence of that sweet and radiant face, and that lithe girlish form.

Lochlin, not a moment too soon, and yet I confess, too, not a moment too late, came from "The King's Parlour," and strolled along the ledge to join me where I stood, torch in hand, hard by the entrance. Together we stood watching, while the slow minutes crawled by. `For more than half-an-hour now the cave was effectually open, yet from the outer world came no token. I had thought my companion heartless. Now he laid his hand on my arm, and said—

"Ere the way is barred I shall swim out and ashore."

I wrung his hand in silence. What would I not have given at that moment to have acquired in my boyhood the common art of swimming?

Presently he announced that he was about to set out for the shore. It was nearly a mile distant, but he was no doubt a good swimmer. We proceeded together towards the alcove where we had passed the night. Here he began to throw off his outer clothes and boots preparatory to taking the water. Suddenly he raised his hand and cried, "Hark." I listened, and heard the muffled sound of many voices. A boat filled with men, doubtless our enemies, was making its way through the rock-corridor which led into the cave. Then the black bows of a boat emerged into the dimly lighted spaces of the water-floor. It was too late for me now to deal with this boat as I had dealt with the other. Just then I heard, in Gaelic, a rough voice cry—

"Here the thief bides; I see a light."

Together we ran to "The King's Parlour," remembering the weapons which were there.

O

"I hope these pistols are loaded," I said, taking some down from the shelf.

"They are," said Lochlin; "I examined them. They are loaded with ball, and the priming is fresh and dry."

"Can you shoot straight?" I said.

"I am a dead shot," he replied.

"Then I shall give you light to shoot by. You take the pistols."

From below I heard some one cry, "Give a light there. Zounds, but 'tis dark."

"*Hanim an dhoul*" (Soul to the devil), cried a second voice, "is it to make a cockshot of ourselves? How do you know the thief hasn't pistols?"

Lochlin and I now arranged our plan of attack. I was to approach the ledge, and project a torch so as to illuminate the water, while avoiding the return fire from the boat. Lochlin was to stand at a distance from me, sheltered in darkness, and do what execution he could. The babbling of voices was still going on beneath us when I heard the first report of Lochlin's pistols, and some one immediately below me remark in a strangely quiet and almost surprised tone of voice,

"Faith, I'm shot." I looked down, but that moment two tongues of fire flashed from the boat, and I was aware that the ledge, less than a foot on my right, had been splintered. The fragments struck me, luckily not in the face. At once I withdrew; I was the torch-bearer on this occasion, not the fighting man.

Again Lochlin fired. He stood, darkling, on my left, between me and the entrance, and shifted his position after every shot.

"Another hit," he cried; "I shall pick them off one by one—if I have time."

The rapparees were certainly brave enough.

I could hear them furiously attempting to swarm the cliff beneath me, and perpetually tumbling back into the boat. They did not discover that fissure by which I had made the ascent, and the light of my torch did not extend so far as to illuminate the shingle.

To Lochlin's last remark he added, "The rascals are going."

"Drop your pistols," I cried; "serve them as I served you."

"But this pistol-practice is so pretty."

"Obey orders," I roared.

The hubbub of voices still sounded below,

but I knew that the boat was escaping. This should not be permitted; for the crew would carry with them the knowledge of our place of concealment, and we would be next besieged by the Barretts and all their rapparees.

I could see Lochlin's form dimly stealing along the ledge to that levelled platform where was the pyramid of great pebbles. Once again I showed myself, but was not fired at; the boat's crew seemed now to be struck by panic, and endeavouring to escape as fast as they could from this trap. Dimly I made out the outline of Lochlin's figure above the entrance, the stone poised in both hands above his head. Then I heard a crash. A moment's silence ensued, during which, like Sheela, I dashed the torch into the water. Then there broke forth a howl. Let the rest be silence.

"Do you think any will escape?"

"No," came the reply, "they are all inland men."

"Show a light there, and I'll make sure," cried a strange voice. It rang hoarsely-furious, reverberating through the long cavern, dominating the yells and moans of those who drowned or still struggled in the water.

Never, not in the hottest battle, had I ever heard a voice so charged with passion.

"Who shouts ?" I cried.

"Conahar MacArdell," replied the voice.

I fired another torch, and standing on the ledge held it on high. Well I knew the bloody work which was now toward on the darkly gleaming water. I saw below me an athletic figure crouched in a curragh. With the left hand he sculled the curragh, in the right he held a glittering sword. So sculling, he darted hither and thither over the water-floor of the cavern with amazing velocity, and ever and anon plunged downwards with his weapon. Then he paused and looked around, but almost at once rushed straight for, and even through, the entrance. Presently he was back again, sculling this time in a direct line towards the shingle.

"And that last," he cried up to me hoarsely as he passed, "that last was the best, big Brian Roe O'Flaherty. He flogged three men till they died ; and as for the women that he——. God in high heaven, but my heart is a dancing star this night. But oh !" he cried again, with a wail in his voice—"but oh! my grief! my grief! (*ma vrone! ma vrone!*) for I was forgetting. Sir, gentlemen, for Christ his sake make haste now, for the tide is coming."

Like a deer or wild goat of the mountains he came bounding up the ragged ledge from the shingle.

"Sir," he said, as he joined us, and speaking with the utmost rapidity, "we must enter Dun-Randal this night, or my dear mistress and sister, the pearl of the world, is worse than lost, and we are worse than all damned, for the Barretts have her. They took her in my grandmother's house—Enoch Barrett and eight of his best men did—and I was alone there with my bit of steel, and couldn't stir, for they would have ended me between them right soon, and that would have been the end of all. And the secret of 'The King's Parlour' is to be dragged from her this night on the rack. My own ears heard them say it, and that will be the parting of body from soul to her, for proud and high is that brave heart. And 'tis I know the way of the tunnel, for I heard it when 'twas told to her. And for Christ's sake, gentlemen, delay not, but to the curragh, and I'll be with you in a flash."

So saying, he darted from us into "The King's Parlour," where lighted candles still burned, and we, saying not a word, ran to the shingle.

We had scarcely arrived there when Conahar was upon us like a whirlwind, with a sheaf of swords gleaming under his arm. These he cast into the curragh, and cried, "Take the sculls, your honour." This to O'Mally. "I'll swim and hold on."

In another moment we were rushing across the water-floor to the cave's mouth, Conahar swimming behind, holding on to the stern with one hand, while he swam with the other so as to increase the speed. I still held the torch. That heap of swords glistening at my feet indicated that brave Conahar was at the head of a small party with whom he purposed assailing the castle. We passed through the entrance and into the open air.

The night was fine and starry, the surface of the sea still. The swash of the curragh as it rushed through the water, bounding forward like a greyhound, the creaking and straining of the sculls, were, I suppose, the

only sound for miles around. We were silent.
This was a race for life. The expression of
O'Mally's pale, set face as he rowed was
tragical in its intensity. Between us and the
shore the sea was clear. Before me, jet black
against the white sands, I saw again the
sinister tower ; red lights in it glowed here and
there. Impelled by Lochlin's sinewy arms
the little curragh bounded shorewards like an
arrow.

"You have half-a-dozen helpers," I said to
Conahar.

"Yes, sir, stout and hardy, three of them
fresh from the wars. But we'll want God's
help too, for there's a power of their best men
now in the castle."

I sat in the stern. Conahar's hand was
beside me on the gunwale. I did not see his
face, but I blessed every red hair of his valiant
and faithful head as it glowed there so
strangely in the bright moonlight. Conversation did not seem to relax his exertions.

"How did that second boat find us ?" I
asked.

"In one of the three boats that hunted you,"
he replied, "there was a sharp lad, who said

you never got away from Lan Bran, and they
laughed at him.   And when Enoch Barrett
himself rowed round the island, and went on
to it, and said there was never a cave or a
cleft in Lan Bran, there was no one to hold
with him.   But the sharp lad stuck to his
notion like wax, and at long last he got a boat
and crew ; but his sharpness did not profit him
or them—*avaceo*, it did not ! "

When we landed, Conahar led us straight
to a point midway between Baronscourt,
described in the first chapter, and the sand.
Here he searched for and found some mark
known only to himself.   Then he whistled,
and half-a-dozen dark figures glided from
under the trees and joined us.   They brought
with them a ladder and the trunk of a fir-tree,
also spades and pick-axes, and a cluster of
bog-wood torches steeped in oil.   Under Conahar's directions the men dug—dug furiously.
Presently a pick rang hard against stone.   A
few minutes later and they had raised a flag
about three feet square, disclosing a dark
passage with   steps   leading   downwards.
Reaching the foot of this flight, and lighting
our torches, we found ourselves in an artificial

subterranean gallery, which ran straight to
the east. I saw that this gallery probably
followed the course of that line of castles,
traces of whose ruins were visible on the sands
above.

CHAPTER XX

THROUGH DARKNESS TO THE DARK TOWER

SUDDENLY we came up against a blank wall. This, then, was no thoroughfare or true tunnel running into Dun-Randal, but a blind passage ending so. Had we lost our way ? Impossible. From the foot of that stone flight on to this point we had passed no door on the right or the left, nor any division of ways. Dismay, ascending almost to panic, possessed us. At this moment perhaps Sheela lay on the rack under the torturing hands of those fiends. We looked at one another amazed and confounded.

Then a swift thought like an inspiration sprang into my mind.

"Bring the ram forward," I shouted. "Ram this wall."

It was done. We rammed once. The ram went crashing through, and a whole torrent of masonry rushed down before us. The whole of that seeming solid barrier disappeared, revealing an aperture of exactly the same size as the gallery which we were traversing. The wall was a mere blind and sham, not a foot thick, and rudely constructed. Just then a sound like the clanking of chains struck my ear, but I did not heed it. When my men were about to rush forward again I restrained them. The noise made by the falling masonry was suspicious. Some fell at our feet, but some of it, I felt sure, fell clattering down into depths. Yes, immediately below where that wall stood there was an abyss. We stood upon its edge and held our torches forward and downward. Before us stretched a great hall of unknown length, for its sides and arched roof were only visible to a short distance in the flare of the torchlights. Beyond, all was darkness. The gallery out of which we had emerged struck this great hall about midway between the roof and floor. There was a narrow ledge here upon which we stood, just beyond and on each side of that aperture which was like a window looking down into the hall. Having gauged the depth, I ordered the ladder to be lowered.

Again I heard that distant clank of irons. My attention was now momentarily diverted to the behaviour of Conahar MacArdell, who stood on the ledge by my side craning out over the abyss with extended torch. His face was pale, his eyes ablaze, his red hair glowing in the torchlight seemed to be in confused motion. He was evidently labouring under some great excitement. I heard him moan continuously. Suddenly, with a cry, but no articulate word, he sprang from the ledge, rolled over on the ground beneath, but rose unhurt, and disappeared into the darkness.

"What is that?" said O'Mally.

"I can guess," I answered; "Conahar has found his master."

I now remembered the basket and rope which I had seen in the lame giant's hand when on that first night I penetrated, an unwelcome visitor, to the basement of Dun-Randal. In this dungeon the Barretts held their prisoner. The significance of that rope and basket was evident. The prisoner's food was let down to him from the cellars of the castle, the floor of the dungeon being at much lower level than the castle basement.

Somewhere in the darkness I now heard broken Gaelic ejaculations and sobbings, and the sound of kisses. Yes, it was quite plain that Conahar had discovered his dear master. We found them still in each other's arms.

"Enough, enough, Conahar. Restrain yourself. Be a man," I heard a young voice cry imperatively. The voice was curiously like Sheela's. Conahar's master and foster-brother, the Baron de Stanton, was a slender youth, very fair, and of a beauty almost feminine. His looks notwithstanding, I was to find later on that he had plenty of spirit. Conahar, whom he had with difficulty repelled, was now kneeling before him, sobbing and kissing passionately one of his master's gyved hands. The young baron turned to us. Though a mere lad and in irons, he bore himself with a certain dignity.

"Gentlemen," he said, "lose not one moment with me. My sister is even now in the cellars of Dun-Randal, where the Barretts are putting her to the torture of the rack. Yes, you will need both ram and ladder. When you ascend from this dungeon you will find a narrow passage. There is but one door between it and the castle cellars. Burst that open, and then—God and your swords. Go, gentlemen ; I am in irons, and powerless to help."

A few seconds later we were at the eastern end of the immense dungeon, and planted our ladder against the wall where a dark aperture disclosed itself similar to that by which we had entered, and at the same height from the floor. We clambered up, bringing the ram with us and a single torch. Here a second passage awaited us running straight forwards, and resembling that which led from the foot of the stone flight to the great dungeon. I now enjoined perfect silence, and led the way, torch in hand. Presently I heard before me the sound of fierce voices, but not the words used. Silence succeeded, after which a moan.

Not blood in that terrible moment coursed through my veins, but torrent fire. Naturally slow to anger, the deluge of wrath and hatred which then flooded my whole being has been since to me a surprising revelation of myself. A brown rusty door, clamped and riveted, all iron, and strong exceedingly, barred the way. I did not fear it; at that moment I was conscious of the strength of ten men. I leaned my torch against the wall, not without a certain deliberation and absence of external hurry and excitement, while within my heart glowed like a furnace at white heat. I took my place at the head of the ram, and gave the signal with my eyes. Once only we rammed; it was enough. Torn from its bolts and hinges the great iron door fell inward, clanging on the stone floor of the cellar beyond, and revealing what? One glance, not of such duration as the fall of a raindrop from the eaves, has pictured that scene for ever in my memory. Sheela lay supine, extended on that long, low table. Her face was invisible, her arms strained straight above her head, the white forearms whiter than snow shining against the darkness of this inferno. A man—no, a devil—was kneeling beside her on the ground, holding a bar in his hands. I noted his attitude, saw in which direction he turned it. His back was towards me, but his face as he sought to look round was half visible above his shoulder. It was Israel Barrett. Other figures stood around; I noted them not. Not a word I said, or cry cried, as I flew straight upon him. Where I struck

him I know not, know only that one stroke
was enough.   Sheela was moaning at the time,
and knew not, in that torture, that her saviours
and avengers were at hand.   I seized the bar
and reversed it.   The moanings died away.
Gently and deliberately, with a skill at which
I have since wondered, I disengaged her
precious limbs from their fastenings, till she
was quite free.   All this time there raged
round me the sounds of fight.   I attended to
that too, for my mind was preternaturally
clear in those moments.   Swift, prompt, and
resourceful, I seemed to observe and understand all things.   The fighting passed from
me towards and up the stair flight out of the
cellar.   When I retook my sword I heard
the oaths and shouts and the clash of steel
in the great hall above my head.   Hastening
thither I found that my men had cleared the
hall, and driven the ward into the upper portions
of the castle ; they sought to follow, but the
play of swords at the foot of the flight showed
that their path was barred.   I knew what had
happened.   The ward, taken by surprise, had
fled panic-stricken, many before few.   They
were recovering from that panic.   Another

P

moment and they would learn, what was the
fact, that the castle had been forced by a
mere handful of men.   To revive their fears
and gain time for the execution of a purpose
which at that instant flashed into my mind,
I raised my voice to the utmost, and cried in
triumphant tones—

"This way, lads.   Lieutenant, hurry up
your men."   I shouted as if to a great company coming up from the cellars.

I stepped to the castle door.   It was locked.
Underneath the door, between it and the
stone threshold, I inserted the point of my
sword and rammed it home, and bent and
snapped the blade so as to afford no purchase
to those who would extract it.   Meantime my
men were still engaged at the foot of the
stairs.   They could not force their way up
against that sword-play in the narrow entrance,
and to retreat would let loose the savage flood
which was penned up there, and which, to
judge by the angry and swelling roar of voices,
threatened momentarily to burst forth.   I approached my comrades, and cried in their ears—

"Back now to the cellar.   Back, for your
lives.   Trust me."

I went first, being now unarmed; they darted after, and that instant the pent-up flood escaped and surged after. Owing to the pressure from behind those in front fell, so checking the pursuit for a few seconds; the impediment, though momentary, was sufficient.

At the foot of the stone flight into the cellars I stood behind the door, having first abstracted the key and flung it before me. As the last of my comrades passed, I slammed-to the iron door, which locked itself. A moment later, from without, men were hurling their bodies against it, but in vain.

I ordered the rest of my men to retreat, but bade MacArdell and Lieutenant O'Mally attend to the Lady Sheela. They raised between them her apparently insensible form, and bore it swiftly into the passage leading to the dungeon. I was alone now. The hurrying feet of my comrades sounded fainter in that flagged passage. Outside the closed door the storm of oaths had ceased to rage; the foiled rapparees had retired to take counsel, or search the castle for a ram. I cast a swift glance around. At my feet lay a giant carcass in a pool of blood. It was the lame constable's, and no doubt on his person was the key of the great door. There were other bodies hard by. The floor felt wet and slippery under my feet, glowing red in the faint candle-light. Israel lay where he fell. I took a sword from the floor, and passed it through him. One, at least, of my devilish cousins was safe for *home*. Then with the butt - end of a matchlock I smashed in the top of a last of powder, and of two others next it. From a coil of quick-match I cut off with my sword some ten minutes' length, as well as I could judge, one end of which I thrust well into that first barrel, and with the flame of a candle fired the other. Then I hastened into the passage, following my party, and can remember what a joyous clangour the fallen iron door gave forth beneath my trampling feet as I passed. That storm of wrath and battle-fury had now somewhat subsided in my heart. I overtook the rest at the foot of the ladder in the great dungeon. Here I bade Conahar attend to his master, and the lieutenant take command of the rest of the men, and hurry forward with the ladder. I myself took in my arms—who but a lover can know with what joy ?—the still apparently insensible form of my darling. Her head lay in the curve of my right arm. To me her weight was a feather ; for truly if the Almighty had not endowed me with a quick and understanding spirit, He had made me stronger than most men. There was something to my mind miraculous and incredible, nay, something terrible, in all this, that I, even I, should bear in my arms, hold against my beating heart, that radiant and beautiful being. I looked down on her fair, pale face, seen in flashes as the shifting, hurrying torchlights flared by. Her pure bright eyes, full and orbed, were veiled now under their white curtains darkly fringed. Pale and still was her face, but I thought there was some sign of life and motion in her beautiful lips, and rejoiced while I trembled.

As I went I murmured lover's phrases and endearments, never dreaming that she heard. But she did.

" I hear you," she murmured. "You wished to say those things last night, but you were afraid."

"Nay, I have done; I shall not say them again."

"But you may, Hugh," she replied, oh so faintly. "I belong to you now, I suppose, since you saved me. And I am not much hurt, only very weak."

I halted a moment, kneeling on one knee— yes, she was mine now, was she not?—and adjusted her limp, weak arms round my neck.

"Can you hold your hands together there?" I said.

"I think I can," she answered, a faint flush suffusing her cheek as her bare hands touched my neck; she bowed her head forward, concealing her face on my bosom, but only for a moment. Suddenly she looked up at me, and said nothing, but her eyes did, and the pressure of her weak hands, and what they said, I understood. I inclined my head and kissed her.

Yet surely she had suffered more than she was willing, perhaps for my sake, to confess, for once again she swooned. Insensible was that precious form which I bore up the ladder at the west end of the dungeon, and through that first tunnel, and so into the open air.

CHAPTER XXI

PUFF, AND ALL'S OVER

I LOOKED to Dun-Randal. It stood there stark grim and black against the sands white with moonlight, against the starry eastern sky, proud, strong, and minatory, as when first against wild clouds lurid with sunset it had disclosed itself to my wondering eyes. Without, all was serene and still; not so within. Far from that; Dun-Randal to-night was like an outpost of the Pit. The rapparees there knew that we had fired the mine; no doubt they had smelt the odour of the burning match. They knew that Death in one of his most frightful forms was momentarily drawing nearer. Escape was impossible, save, perhaps, to men having their passions under full control, and, dominated by panic, the inmates of Dun-Randal were now a horde of raving, raging, and howling maniacs.

Hard by a rock jutted from the lawn. I bore Sheela thither, and leaned her against it.

"What frightful noise is that?" she asked faintly.

"You will know presently, darling," I said; "and do not be alarmed if you hear the sound of a great explosion."

I turned again to Dun-Randal. For one swift moment an emotion of pity shook me as the full meaning of that agony filled my mind, but it was swept away in other thoughts. What if my train had missed fire? What, then, would be our fate? What Sheela's?

A dark figure started now from the clear sky outline of the battlements. To his mouth he set something that shone. Anon the shrilling of a trumpet rose clear above that howl of despairing souls. That blare from the battlements hardly ceased for an instant, and added a strange element of terror to the scene. Others swiftly followed, and fired pieces. They were signalling for help to their comrades in the town. That summons was heard, for answering shouts arose there, red lights multiplied, and dusky, quick-moving figures began to dot the white sand.

The moon, nearly full, hung in the north-west, and illuminated the landward-looking front of Dun-Randal. Brighter moonlight and starlight I have seldom seen ; it was near as bright as day. Some of those running figures ran back to announce, I believe, that the castle door was shut. Then the main body of rapparees broke from the village. They were apparently under some sort of control, for I heard strong words of command. In their midst they bore a long tree or beam withal to burst the castle door. What was their interpretation of this sudden hell which had broken loose in the Black Tower ? A mutiny ? A quarrel amongst the ward, even-tuating in mutual slaughter ? The nocturnal irruption into their stronghold of that myste-rious foe which, having already destroyed two boats' crews, had, by equally mysterious means, gained an entrance to the castle, secured the outlet, and, in superior numbers, were now slaughtering their comrades ? I cannot tell. Plain enough it was to them that Death in some frightful shape was busy to-night in the Black Tower, for the trumpet sounded continually from the battlements, and the

intermittent flashes of fire and reports of
guns there, and the terrible howling which
never for one instant ceased, told the same
tale. Of the imprisoned rapparees some now
leaped from the turrets and upper windows.
Three such I saw go headlong, but they never
stirred from the place where they fell. They
lay there, black splashes on the white sand. I
now saw something grey and fluttering let
down from the parapets, growing longer by
degrees. Some of the ward not quite over-
whelmed and swept away in the madness of
the hour, were constructing a means of descent by joined bedclothes or draperies.

But now when I looked to see men descend
by the same, none did. On the battlements,
where the upper end of this improvised rope
was knotted round one of the turrets of the
machicolated parapet, a mass of frantic hu-
manity swayed to and fro. There I saw raised
hands, and the murderous glittering of short
steel. Where every one strove to descend
first, none could descend at all.

Then above that tumult, above the hoarse
clamour of the onrushing relief and the howl
from within the Black Tower, I heard another

sound, shrill and piercing, dominating all that
confused uproar.   High, ecstatic, cleaving the
night like a sword, rose a woman's scream,
and yet not a scream, rather a cry of infinite
triumph and exultation.   It came from that
lonely watcher by the quicksands.   This was
her Day of Judgment.   Perhaps she did see
"the Lord" descending visibly to take vengeance on the Great Dhoul and his children
and his host.   And that scream rang, and
never ceased to ring, over the wild scene
down to the catastrophe which fast drew
nigh.

For now that dusky cohort from the village
were poured round the north front, and
rammed the castle door.   I could see the line
of strong men where they slowly retreated
and rushed forwards again with fierce but
ordered impetuosity, could hear the hoarse
voice of some one in authority there, and the
crash and clang of breaking timber and shiv-
ering steel.   Three times altogether they
rammed ; at the fourth impact the great door
flew open.   There was a momentary struggle
in the porch and doorway, after which the
crowd from without poured inwards, by their

superior weight and numbers sweeping before them those who from the interior sought an exit. The clamour and uproar, the prevailing panic and excitement, had effectually drowned the voices of those, if any, who being within shouted a warning to those who were without. The battlements were quite deserted from the moment when the exterior rapparees with their battering ram drew nigh to the castle. All the ward seemingly had rushed down that they might escape through the open door, a hope of which they were frustrated. Nevertheless, now on the deserted battlements, struggling up out of the crowd which from above surged into the interior of the castle, one small but active figure reappeared. It was closely followed, almost pursued, by a taller, younger, and more athletic. Of this second man, the splendidly formed head and shoulders showed clear against the starry sky. What a background! Of the identity of those two figures, the pursuer and the pursued, figures which still, in pallid and stricken moods, haunt my memory and imagination with a sense of cruel nightmare as of a momentary vision of the Pit, I have never entertained a doubt. They were Sir Theodore Barrett and his eldest son. I saw the small man seize that improvised and fluttering rope with one hand, while with face upturned to the other he seemed to deprecate wrath, or urge an entreaty in vain. A blow, quick as lightning, was the only response. He fell within the battlements, and the tall man, with a certain deliberate speed, seizing the rope, prepared to descend. But it was not the purpose of the great and just God that His holy earth should ever again upbear those parricidal feet. For now the great Black Tower rocked as if shaken to and fro by unseen giant hands. Simultaneously the loopholes and windows glowed red. Then one crimson rent like a tongue of flame darting from above downwards clove the black western front, and like a huge fan suddenly unfolded the explosion burst forth. Vast masses of masonry showed black in the red heart of the explosion, masses not so great in the paler outside glow; some, still smaller, were hurled upwards into the clear starry spaces. Then a sound smote the ear, not clear or detonating, but horribly dull, and more horrible so. The ground quaked beneath my feet, and I fell to the earth.

When I looked again Dun-Randal was no more. A ruinous heap showed where the grim tower stood, while black masses and fragments of masonry dotted the white sand far and wide. A thick, leaden-coloured canopy of smoke was slowly lifting, bluish-black, solid-seeming, blotting out the stars, slowly, very slowly, peacefully, very peacefully, moving to the zenith, paling as it rose. Below, all was silence. The trumpeting, the gunshots, the calls, the noise of deadly strife, the howlings of despair, the cries of those who ran, the thunderous clangour of the ram, that terrible scream—all had ceased. A perfect silence reigned where that horrid tumult had so late seemed to fill the world. I heard near by the gentle wash of waves, and the slumberous murmur of the great deep. Somewhere inland, unseen torrents, faintly musical, little silver bells in the hills. One luminous star in the east, of peerless splendour and beauty, hitherto concealed by the dark tower, shone now with living and palpitating light. It was the morning star.

I turned to Sheela where she lay, pale, motionless, gazing on the black ruins and the gleaming sand.   Her eyes, filled with starlight, looked strangely large and solemn.

"They are all dead," I said—"dead, and in Hell."

"They are in God's hands," she replied.

I kneeled down beside her; I took her weak hands in mine and gently restored them to their former place round my neck. With one bright smile, such as all the wealth of the wide world could not purchase, and one low cry, she hid her face on my bosom.

"O Hugh, I am so happy, so happy," she murmured.   "If only my dear, dear brother—if only Raymond—but what is that noise?"

"Lie still a moment, darling; promise me that you will?   It is only Conahar filing through the gyves with which they bound him."

"Bound whom?"

"Your brother, the Baron Raymond de Stanton."

.   .   .   .   .   .

" But your treasure, grandpapa ? "

" My treasure ! why, as I have just told you, I held her in my arms."

" But we mean your gold, your guineas, grandpapa."

" Bother your guineas. I tell you again, my treasure was in my arms."

POSTSCRIPT BY THE EDITOR

I THINK Lieutenant Netterville's narrative, from this forward, may better be left to the imagination. And yet, in these days of treasure-stories, it may be as well to add that, amongst the débris of Dun-Randal scattered over the strand next morning, between the ruins of Dun-Randal and that creek towards the west, from which, on the night of the escape, Conahar's trampling feet had sent up those diamond-bright showers, Sir Theodore's strong iron treasure - chest was discovered quite by itself, a good deal battered and bent, but unbroken. After satisfying from the contents all just claims, including those of our hero and of the poor maltreated peasantry upon his estates, Raymond de Stanton, by courtesy styled the Baron, distributed the remainder amongst the nearest discoverable relatives of Sir Theodore, who were for the most part poor persons residing in different parts of Connaught.

Q

Of the rapparees, one boy and six men only escaped. Amongst the latter was Ancient Byrne, who happened to be somewhat indisposed at the time when the alarm was given. Though he certainly deserved the rope rather than anything else, Lieutenant Netterville and the Lady Sheela thought good to grant the old sinner a small annuity, which, surprising to relate, he lived to enjoy for a good many years. Ancient Byrne continued to reside in that village at the strand's head, of which village he became rather an ornament, and where he opened a fencing school. One of the very few gentlemen who ever drew blood from "Tiger" Roche confessed that he had received his first lessons in swordsmanship from Felim-na-Cogga, that is to say, Felim of the Dice.

STANDISH O'GRADY.

Printed by BALLANTYNE, HANSON & Co
Edinburgh and London